JACK'S SECRET
WORLD

JACK'S SECRET WORLD

JACK RYDER

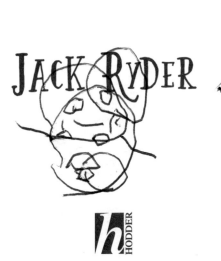

h HODDER

HODDER CHILDREN'S BOOKS

First published in Great Britain in 2021 by Hodder and Stoughton

1 3 5 7 9 10 8 6 4 2

Text copyright © Jack Ryder, 2021
Illustrations copyright © Alice McKinley, 2021

The moral rights of the author and illustrator have been asserted.

A CIP catalogue record for this book
is available from the British Library.

ISBN 978 1 44495 299 5

Printed and bound in Great Britain by Clays Ltd.

The paper and board used in this book are from
well-managed forests and other responsible sources.

Hodder Children's Books
An imprint of
Hachette Children's Group
Part of Hodder & Stoughton
Carmelite House
50 Victoria Embankment
London EC4Y 0DZ

An Hachette UK Company
www.hachette.co.uk

www.hachettechildrens.co.uk

For Ella and Marnie

PROLOGUE

A secret can be a very powerful thing. Who knows, you may have even come across one before … Perhaps you were told one by a wrinkly old grandparent? Or maybe you heard the tiny whisperings of one in the playground at school?

Like many things in this world, secrets can come in all shapes and sizes. Some are big, some are only small. Some are dark, and some shine with bright colours. Some are dangerous and some have curious truths and some are just too crazy and ridiculous to understand!

As you probably already know, most secrets don't stay *secrets* for very long. More often than not they are whispered to another person, and then to another, and then another, until soon the whole town is gossiping about it and nobody can remember it was even a secret in the first place!

Now, lean in a little closer because there is something very important I have to tell you ...

Some secrets are extra special. Because *some* secrets are *magical* ... and if you look carefully, you might just find one within the pages of this book ... though how long the boy who discovered it will be able to keep it a secret is another matter altogether ...

DAY STARS

Jack squeezed his eyes closed tightly as he, Bruno, Rocco and Dottie stepped through the wall of the old, empty house and into the glimmering, sparkling light of another world.

Now as fun as this sounds, I wouldn't suggest trying this at home, children. It doesn't work with the walls in most houses. You'll just end up banging your head. But as you've probably guessed, this wasn't any old house, and the summer that led up to this moment wasn't any old summer. It had been a summer filled with fun, adventure and —

most exciting of all – *magic*.

The fun had begun when Jack and his new neighbours, Bruno and Rocco Buckley, and their dog, Dottie, went to explore an old empty house, covered in ivy, that used to be owned by Jack's granddad. Inside the house, they found a strange girl with no memory who was looking for her father. The girl was called Blossom, and the boys agreed to help her. Together, they formed a gang – the secret summer gang – and set out to solve the mystery of who the girl was and where her father had gone.

They began by searching the house for clues and soon discovered it was filled with magic, left behind by the girl's father: magical potions, kept in glass bottles, and when you opened them, peculiar and wondrous things started to happen … Rocco found that he could fly like a falcon. Bruno could run as fast as a cheetah. And to their delight, Jack and Blossom were able to talk to animals.

But most exciting of all, the ivy that covered the house, both inside and out, was itself magical, and when there was a storm, the rain watered it and turned one of the ivy-covered walls into a doorway to another world.

It was this doorway that Blossom had gone through some time earlier, looking for her father, and it was this doorway that Jack, Bruno, Rocco and Dottie were stepping through now, in pursuit of her. Jack couldn't leave Blossom now. He had promised to help her find her dad. And, well, there was another reason he needed to find her, a secret reason that only Jack knew. But we'll come back to that. For now, we'd better step through the doorway too ...

With his eyes still closed, Jack took another step, and stopped. The storm that had been raging all around him in his world suddenly ceased to exist. The rumbling thunder and howling winds faded away and were replaced by a vast quietness.

Jack could feel the ground beneath his feet had turned soft. It felt like … grass. And was that a gentle ray of sun he could feel against his cheeks?

Very slowly, Jack dared to open his eyes and what an amazing sight it was that met him.

All around him was a world of green country. There was green grass and green fields stretching out as far as the eye could see, dotted all over with bright yellow buttercups, just like the ones that were growing inside the old empty house, and above it all was the most extraordinary sight – an enormous rainbow-coloured sky that was filled with stars, even though it was clearly the middle of the day!

Just then a swarm of bumble bees came hovering past singing a tune.

'We love it when it's sunny,
We sing because it's funny,
We're off to get the honey,
To fill our furry tummies.'

Jack laughed at their funny song.

'Did you hear that?' he asked Bruno and Rocco.

'Hear what?' Bruno shouted back.

It must still be the magic, thought Jack. Now that he could understand what they were saying, Jack wondered if bees always sang like this. He watched them fly over to a small tree standing in the middle of the field. There was bright sparkling fruit hanging from its branches and the glorious colours from the sky made the whole thing twinkle like a Christmas tree.

'Apricots!' barked Dottie.

Jack looked down and saw Bruno and Rocco's dog, Dottie, rubbing up against his legs, wagging her tail excitedly. 'See? I told you I could smell apricots!' she barked up at him, then went chasing after the bees.

'Come on, Jack!' Rocco shouted, waving Jack over to the tree. Beyond him Bruno was climbing the tree already and reaching out to grab one of the sparkling apricots.

'These are delicious!' Bruno shouted down. He was hanging from a branch chewing away happily, with enormous hamster cheeks filled with fruit. He tossed one of the sparkling apricots to Jack.

'Hey, where's mine?' cried Rocco.

'Get it yourself, you lazy bum,' Bruno called down to him cheekily.

Jack offered a bite of his apricot to Rocco, but Rocco waved it away and began instead to magically rise off the ground. Even though Jack had seen him do this a few times now, it still gave him a shock every time.

Rocco flew up into the tree, plucked a juicy apricot from one of the branches and took a great bite out of it.

'Mmmmm ... so sweet!' said Rocco between bites. 'Come on, Jack, climb up and join us!' Rocco shouted down.

Jack climbed up and joined the brothers. The three of them sat there, perched on the tree's thick branches, happily munching on the wonderfully sweet fruit and looking out over the view. They all gasped as a chorus of shooting stars glided silently over their heads.

'What sort of place has stars in the daytime?' Rocco was saying curiously as he looked up squinting at the magnificent sky.

'I love it,' said Bruno, gazing upward. 'It

feels like we're in another galaxy!'

From up there they could see right across the field and down into a beautiful valley. At the bottom was a river with crystal blue water flowing through the middle of it, and along the riverbank there was a whole mass of pink blossom trees. Beyond the valley, resting peacefully on the horizon, Jack could see a spectacular waterfall. A thin needle of sparkling water was flowing all the way down it and as it reached the bottom it exploded, sending clouds of rainbow-coloured mist into the air.

Jack knew he was awake but there was a very real part of him that felt he was asleep inside a mysterious dream.

'Do you think we'll be able to get back?' asked Bruno, glancing over his shoulder towards the shimmering curtain of ivy.

'Get back?' Rocco blurted out through a mouthful of apricot. 'Why would we want to get back? This place is awesome!'

Bruno sighed and turned to Jack, hoping for a more intelligent response.

Jack thought for a moment. 'First we need to find Blossom,' he said. 'Then we'll figure out how to get back home.'

'How are we going to find her?' asked Bruno. 'She could be anywhere.'

Jack stared out over the green fields and didn't know where to start. She could have gone in any number of directions in search of her dad.

'We should split up,' Jack said at last. 'Then we'll have a better chance of finding her.'

'Good idea, Jacky-boy,' said Bruno. 'I'll whizz across these fields. I can cover lots of ground that way.'

'And I can fly over to the other side of the valley,' said Rocco.

'Fine,' said Jack. 'I'll walk down to the

river with Dottie. Maybe she can use her sense of smell to track Blossom down.'

Dottie jumped up with her paws resting against the trunk of the tree and barked excitedly. 'I'm ready!' she said. 'Let's go!'

'We have to be careful though,' Jack said. 'We don't know what this place is yet.'

There was a short pause.

'What do you mean?' Bruno asked him.

'Well I know it all looks wonderful and everything,' Jack said, 'but we don't know anything about this world. We don't even know what lives here …'

Bruno leaned into Jack with a very serious look in his eyes. 'You mean like lions and stuff?' he said.

Jack felt a cold shiver slide up the back of his neck and said, 'Yes, possibly …'

'Ah great!' said Rocco, reaching for another apricot. 'No one said we were gonna get eaten by lions! I didn't sign up for this!'

'*You* won't get eaten,' said Bruno, raising his voice. 'You can fly! All you have to do is fly up into the air and nothing can touch you.'

'Oh yeah,' said Rocco more cheerfully. 'What about you though?'

'I can just zoom off!' said Bruno, folding his arms confidently. 'I've got cheetah speed! Cheetahs are faster than lions so I'll just outrun them if they come anywhere near me!'

'And what about me?' Jack asked a little more fearfully.

'I guess you'll just have to try and talk your way out of it,' said Bruno, chuckling.

'Yeah good luck with that!' Rocco said, slapping him on the back.

'Last one back to the apricot tree's a loser!' yelled Bruno as the Buckleys disappeared, leaving Jack and Dottie alone.

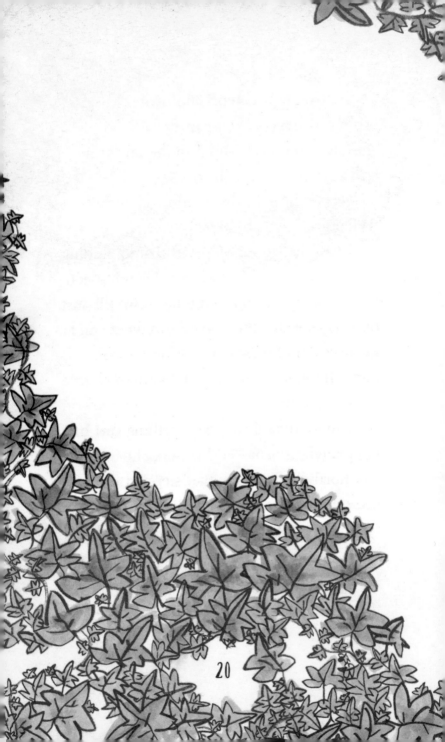

20

THE RIVER

Dottie was already running towards the river as Jack climbed down from the tree. He followed on after her but he didn't run. His mind had become tangled with questions and he was grateful to have a moment on his own to think through everything that had happened.

Shortly before Jack had stepped through the doorway looking for Blossom, he had discovered a secret – a secret that only he knew. He wanted to tell Bruno and Rocco, but he didn't know if they would believe him. It was just too crazy. But however crazy it was, he also knew that it was true. Blossom's missing dad, who the gang had set out to help her find, had turned out to be none other than Jack's granddad. This could only mean one thing – that Blossom was his mum. Jack's mum had gone missing when Jack was only a toddler and nobody knew where she'd gone. Jack was now convinced that some of his granddad's crazy magic had somehow turned her back into a girl and made her lose her memory. His only hope of getting his mum back was to find his granddad, but where to look?

Jack followed Dottie's wagging tail down to the riverbank, at last catching her up. They weaved in and out through the forest of pink blossom trees. Everything around them seemed so unspoiled and untouched. Looking ahead, Jack could see the river flowing all the way down towards a small bridge.

'Keep close, Dottie,' Jack said as he scanned the trees and when he opened his mouth to speak again a crowd of orange butterflies came fluttering towards them from across the river. There must have been a thousand of them. Jack watched in wonder as they all suddenly stopped directly in front of them.

'Hello,' said one of the tiny voices.

Jack smiled at them nervously.

'You look like you've lost something,' said another tiny voice in the flittering crowd.

'We're looking for a little girl,' said Jack. 'Have you seen her?'

'We haven't, I'm afraid,' squeaked another butterfly. 'But we did just fly past a hut in the forest.'

'A hut?' said Jack excitedly. 'Where?'

The butterflies all began swarming around each other, creating the shape of an enormous arrow. It pointed straight across the river and into the forest from which they came.

'It was through there just beyond those trees!' the butterflies all chanted together.

Jack stared into the forest and noticed a thin line of smoke rising out of the tops of the trees.

'Thank you for your help!' said Jack.

'We are glad to be of assistance,' came another tiny voice. 'Now we must press on. We're migrating to the southern mountain today and we cannot fail in our mission.'

'I totally understand,' said Jack with a nod to his new friends.

As all the butterflies hurried away, Jack and Dottie continued on towards the bridge.

When they got closer, Jack could see that the bridge was a makeshift one, made out of a few branches tied together with old rope. It was quite narrow, and it had to be a good ten metres to the other side – and the drop down

to the river below was at least double that. A nervous feeling pinched at Jack's throat.

'I'll go first,' barked Dottie. She hopped on to the bridge and trotted along the branches with ease. 'Come on!' she barked as she lay down on the grass on the other side. 'Your turn!'

Jack crept forward slowly and stepped on to the bridge. It seemed sturdy enough, and with his arms stretched out wide he began to edge his way across. He had nearly made it to the other side when suddenly – *CRACK!* A branch snapped beneath Jack's feet, and he lost his footing and slipped. It all happened in a flash and before Jack knew it, his legs were dangling above the fast-moving river below, his fingers clinging on desperately to the remaining branch.

'HELP!' he screamed. Dottie barked and barked, but there was nothing either of them could do.

'I can't hold on any more!' said Jack,
staring down in terror at the rushing water
below. Just as he was about to lose his grip,
from out of nowhere a large strong
hand suddenly grabbed him and
yanked him upwards
a w a y

from the water, then deposited him face down on to the riverbank.

Jack's heart was pounding as he saw two great big boots standing in front of him. Straining his neck, Jack looked up at a large bearded man in a long dark coat.

The beard was huge and wild, like it hadn't been cut in decades, and the face it belonged to was ancient. But it was his eyes that really caught Jack's attention. In amongst this wild storm of a face, deeply set behind everything else, rested two blue eyes as bright as stars.

Jack pulled himself up to a seated position as he gazed at the mysterious figure. Was this strange-looking man the person they had been searching for? Was this Blossom's dad? Jack's grandfather?

Jack felt Dottie tenderly licking his hand. She then looked up at the man and barked,

'What a nice man! He saved you! He smells like Blossom!'

The old man leaned forward and said, 'Did you say Blossom?'

Jack stared up at the old man in shock. 'You can hear her?' he said.

'Of course I can hear her!' the old man chuckled. 'She's stood right there, isn't she? I might be old but I'm not deaf, you know!'

His voice was mighty and deep and his whole face seemed to brighten with laughter as if this was the funniest thing he'd heard in years.

'Now, did I hear you say Blossom?'

Jack dusted himself off and got to his feet. 'Yes, Blossom's here. I'm looking for her,' said Jack. 'I'm Jack, I'm–' He paused before adding quietly, 'I think I'm your grandson.'

GRANDDAD

The old man didn't speak for some time. He seemed to have been struck dumb by this news. Then all of a sudden a great noise exploded out of him.

'Good golly gosh!' he cried, slapping a giant hand against his forehead. 'I haven't seen you since you were no taller than my knee!' He was looking at Jack in absolute wonderment and Jack could see there was a great big smile hidden beneath that enormous beard of his.

'You'd better come in,' he said, walking off into the forest without waiting for an answer.

'You can tell me everything!'

Jack scrambled to his feet and hurried after the strange old man. He could now see the hut that the butterflies had mentioned, and he followed his granddad into it. The hut was so small, it looked like a tiny tree house that had crash landed to the ground. Inside, the old man had placed some dry twigs on to a small wood-burning stove in the middle of the floor and motioned for Jack to sit. Beneath that long dark coat of his, Jack noticed his granddad was wearing a thick knitted jumper with lots of holes in it. His trousers were baggy and smeared with mud and his gigantic leather boots were wide open with no laces.

'How's Blossom? When did you get here? Did you get the magic I sent?' asked Granddad excitedly. 'Too many questions! Well, you'd better start at the beginning …'

So Jack explained about how he and Bruno and Rocco had gone to explore the old empty house one day, and how they'd found a little girl there with no memory, who was looking for her dad, and how by following the clues in the house, and talking to the animals at the Retirement Home for Old Animals where they soon realised that Blossom's dad must have worked, somehow they had figured out where he had disappeared to.

'But it was only after Blossom had gone after you that I worked out that you must be my granddad, and she was, you know …' Jack finished lamely.

'Oh dear, oh dear,' said Granddad, staring down into the fire. 'So she's been missing all that time? And she has no memory of being anything but nine years old? She must have found the bottle from the bakery. The magic must be stronger than I'd thought.'

'Yes, that's right,' said Jack. 'She had the bottle when we found her. It says "Blossom at the bakery age nine" on the label.'

'Yes, that's the one,' said Granddad, shaking his head. 'Oh dearie me.'

'What was in it?' asked Jack, who was on the edge of his seat now. 'Did the magic come from an animal like the other bottles?'

'I'll explain on the way. There isn't time now. First we must find her, and get you all back before the doorway closes again. Now, where did you appear?'

'What do you mean?' asked Jack.

'When you came through the doorway, where did you appear?' Granddad asked as he stamped out the fire with his huge boot. 'Was there a memorable landmark? Something you remember seeing?'

'There was an apricot tree,' answered Jack. 'That's where we came through the ivy.'

'Well, there's only one apricot tree in

these parts!' Granddad cried. 'Delicious apricots they are too! We'd better head there right away … Blossom's a clever girl. She's bound to head back there too.' With great long strides the old man glided out of the hut and back to the edge of the river with his long coat streaming out behind him, and Dottie trotting along happily at his ankles.

'How do we get back across the river?' asked Jack, finding himself having to run quite fast just to keep up.

'I made another bridge further upstream!' said Granddad. 'Hopefully this one won't snap under your feet! It's this way!'

'My friends might have already found Blossom!' said Jack, still chasing after his granddad. 'They have powers too!'

'Powers, eh?' Granddad said. 'I take it you used my bottles then?'

'Yes we did!' panted Jack. 'Rocco can fly

like a falcon and Bruno can run as fast as a cheetah!'

'Oh well then!' his granddad chuckled, glancing back over his shoulder. 'I see there's been all sorts of fun going on whilst I've been away!'

Following Dottie, they quickly crossed the second bridge over the river and charged into the forest of pink blossom trees.

'So you were saying,' reminded Jack, 'about the bottle Blossom found?'

'Ah yes,' Granddad said, ducking through. 'It was a scent, like a perfume.'

'What was in it?' Jack asked.

'It was a memory,' his granddad said. 'A perfect memory of hers that I captured when she was about your age, I guess. She was eating a great big slice of cake at the bakery. I used to take her there for breakfast.'

'Cake for breakfast?' said Jack, screwing up his face.

'Kids love cake for breakfast!' Granddad cried. 'Doesn't your dad ever take you for cake?'

'Not for breakfast, no!' Jack laughed.

'Well, I'll have to have a word when I see him,' he said with a wink.

Jack tried again to steer the conversation back to what had happened to his mum.

'So how did you capture a memory?' asked Jack politely. 'And if it turned her into a little girl again, can you, you know, reverse it?'

'Well, with some magic, young Jack, it's hard to say,' his granddad told him.

'But you're going to turn her back, aren't you?' Jack said to him. 'When we find her? You'll tell her what happened and make it right again?'

His granddad stopped and turned back to Jack.

'You see the thing is, dear boy,' said

Granddad putting a hand on Jack's shoulder, 'we mustn't tell Blossom who she really is. I know there's probably a part of you that's longing to tell her, but she wouldn't understand.'

Jack stayed silent staring into his granddad's eyes.

'She doesn't know who she was before,' his granddad went on. 'It's like starting from scratch. She only knows who she is *now*.'

'But you CAN fix her, right?' asked Jack. He had only just met this strange old man and didn't know whether he could trust him.

'Don't you worry, young Jack …' said Granddad with another wink. 'Leave everything to me!'

Jack still wasn't sure if he believed him, but before he had a chance to question him more, there was a loud thud and something leapt out of the trees and landed on the ground in front of them. Jack jumped back with a start as it took him a moment to realise who it was.

'Blossom!' he cried.

'Dad!' she screamed, running over to him. 'You're here! You're here!'

'Haha! You jumped out of a blossom tree!' Granddad cried as he whisked her up into the air and gave her the biggest hug in the world. 'My darling girl! My darling girl!' he was saying.

When Granddad placed her back on to the ground, Blossom stood back a bit, looking at him strangely. 'You've gotten OLD!' she said with a frown.

For a split second, Granddad seemed to be lost for words. Then he really looked at her with a smile and said, 'You're just as I remember … I am so happy to see you!'

Jack shuffled around, unsure what to do with himself. He was happy they had found each other. That was what the gang had set out to do, after all. But he couldn't help feeling a little left out.

'Hey, kid!' said Blossom, giving him a friendly dead arm. 'We did it! You found him! And this place! Isn't it incredible? Have you seen all the stars in the sky? I've never seen anywhere as magical as this before!'

Jack opened his mouth to speak but no words came out, so he just smiled. A part of him still desperately wanted to tell Blossom the truth but his granddad had told him not to say anything and leave it to him, so that's what Jack would have to do.

'We have to get going!' said Granddad, hurrying forward again. 'There's even less time to lose now than there was before! Who knows how long the doorway will stay open for …'

Blossom didn't move. She suddenly looked confused.

'But aren't we going to stay here?' she asked.

Granddad paused and turned around. He looked at Blossom, and then at Jack. 'We'll come back, don't worry,' he told Blossom reassuringly. 'But right now, we're going to take young Jack and his friends back through the ivy and get them home. Once we're there, there's just a few things I have to do before we come back. I made a promise to an old friend and I might need your help carrying it out.'

'We'll help you!' Blossom cried. Her whole face was shining with joy again.

'Fantastic!' said Granddad, clapping his giant hands together. He turned to Jack and winked at him. 'What do you say, Jack? Fancy a little adventure?'

Jack didn't know what to say. All Jack

really wanted was his mum back and he couldn't help feel a slight sting of jealousy as he watched Granddad charging on ahead with Blossom. But he had no choice. Jack would just have to wait and go along with his granddad's plans for now, and hope he would make it right in the end.

EGG

Rolling clouds of purple mist now filled the air as the three of them made their way up the hill to the apricot tree. Jack marvelled at the swirling patterns flooding the sky, like ink when it touches water.

Granddad, with Blossom beside him, was marching a metre or so ahead of Jack. Blossom was exploding with energy asking her father all sorts of questions about the night of the storm and why he had gotten so old and grown such a long beard. Jack could almost see the excitement bouncing off her. Granddad attempted to change the

subject a few times, but the questions kept on coming. He looked like a giant next to his daughter as she happily skipped along beside him at a terrific pace. When she ran out of questions, she began telling him all about the secret summer gang and the Buckleys and the magical gobstoppers in the bottles and meeting Jumbo at the animal home.

'I love talking to the animals,' she was jabbering, 'they're just like us, aren't they … Jumbo was really friendly. He told us all about how you and him learned to talk to each other and when you took tears from his eyes and mixed them into magic potions … I also spoke with an emu who needed a haircut, he looked funny … and two seagulls were fighting with each other over a pack of chips … and then I spoke to a giraffe!'

'Calm yourself down, Blossom, or you're going to pop!' Granddad said, looking down at her fondly.

'I know!' she puffed. 'But I am just so happy!'

'I can see that, my dear,' said Granddad patiently. 'But we must try to conserve our energy. There are big plans ahead and we need to be ready with our minds sharp!'

'Plans? Oh I love plans!' cried Blossom, squeezing her hands tightly together.

As they got to the top of the hill, the apricot tree came into view, and there were Bruno and Rocco swinging off the tree like two happy monkeys.

'It's about time!' Bruno called out, chomping away with a mouth full of apricot. 'I see you found her then!'

'Found me?' Blossom cried. 'More like I found them!'

'You must be Blossom's dad!' Rocco shouted down.

'He sure is!' Blossom cheered.

Granddad went and introduced himself to the Buckley brothers. 'A pleasure it is to meet you boys!' he said, seizing Bruno's hand and shaking it with such a terrific force that Bruno almost came tumbling out of the tree.

Just then Dottie started barking. 'Over here!' she barked.

'What is it, girl?' Bruno shouted. 'What have you found?'

The brothers scrambled down from the tree and the gang ran over to see what Dottie was barking at. They found her crouched down and sniffing at something in the undergrowth.

'Is that … an egg?' Rocco said.

'Of course it's an egg, you idiot,' said Bruno. 'What else could it be!'

'It must have fallen out of the tree or something?' said Jack, glancing up into the branches above. There didn't seem to be a nest up there and certainly not one large enough to hold an egg of this size.

'Don't touch it!' Bruno yelled as Rocco moved in closer.

'Why not?' said Rocco.

'Because you don't know who its mother is!' Bruno said cautiously. 'It could be a Komodo dragon for all we know!'

Rocco beamed up at his brother with widening eyes. 'A dragon egg?!' he gasped. 'We could take it home with us!'

Bruno rolled his eyes. 'Take it home with us?' Bruno mocked. 'Oh yeah, Mum and Dad would just love a pet dragon in the house!'

Jack knelt down beside Rocco to take a closer look at the egg. The shell looked as thick as rock and it was big enough that you would need to use two hands to lift it.

'Please can we take it with us?' whispered Rocco, bouncing up and down on his knees as if he had just discovered a hidden birthday present in the cupboard. He leaned forward and gently brushed the egg's surface with the tips of his fingers.

'I think it's best we don't disturb it, Rocco,' said Jack. 'It needs its mum.'

'But what if its mum can't find it?' whispered Rocco sadly. 'We can't just leave it here all by itself.'

Jack had never seen Rocco looking so upset. He laid a hand on Rocco's shoulder and was about to comfort him, when all of a sudden, Granddad's voice rang out. 'Over here, you lot!'

The gang got up and made their way over to Granddad, who was walking slowly towards something. Jack could see a golden sliver of sparkling light piercing through the leaves like a knife. 'There it is!' Granddad whispered, pointing to the light. 'There's the doorway,

right there!'

The gang came over and huddled round him.

'Can you hear it?' Granddad whispered.

Everyone listened carefully as Granddad reached his hands towards the light and slowly parted the curtain of ivy.

Ever so gently, the leaves all around began trembling to the sound of distant thunder.

'It's the storm!' whispered Blossom excitedly.

'Everyone ready for a mission?' said Granddad.

'Mission?' said Bruno, frowning. 'What mission? I thought finding you was the mission?'

'Yes,' said Blossom proudly. 'But now there's a new one!'

'And what is that exactly?' Bruno said, feeling frustrated that he hadn't been told this new piece of information.

Blossom opened her mouth to tell him and then she froze. 'I have no idea,' she said, as if only just realising this. 'What is the mission, Dad?'

'All in good time,' said Granddad. 'Let's get to the other side first and I promise, all will be revealed! Everybody ready?'

The gang all nodded. 'Where's Rocco?' said Jack, noticing he wasn't with them.

'Rocco!' called out his brother.

'Coming!' said Rocco, rushing over to join them.

'You were still messing about with that egg, weren't you?' said Bruno. 'Come on, we need to get home!'

'Want to go first, Jack?' said Granddad, grinning at him through his giant beard.

There was no denying that Jack felt a little bit scared, but he was determined not to show it. 'All right,' he said, stepping forward.

Once again Granddad reached out a long

arm and parted the hanging curtain
of ivy. 'After you.' he said politely, and one
by one they all stepped back through the
doorway.

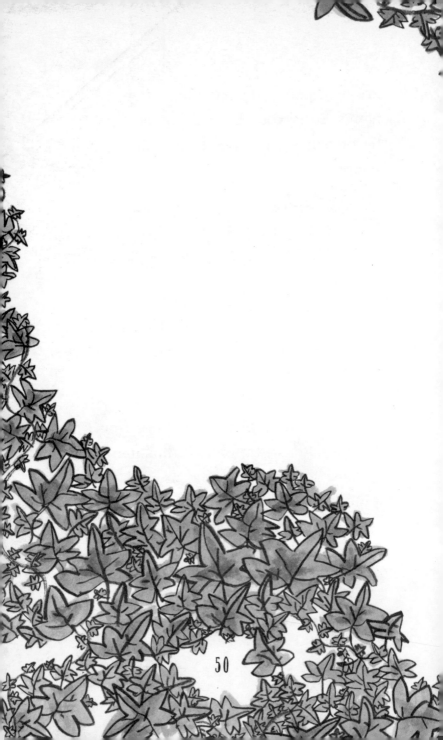

50

HOME

Jack came tumbling through the curtain of ivy, with Blossom right behind him. Together they rolled across the hardwood floor before coming to a stop.

Light had snapped back into darkness and all of the peaceful quietness from the other world had vanished within an instant.

Jack sat up and looked around. It took a moment for his eyes to fully adjust to the gloom, and when they did, he realised he was back inside the old empty house, with its strange ivy-covered walls. The howling winds from the storm were still roaring outside like

iant monsters trying to come
he windows.

as fun!' giggled Blossom, as they
eir feet. Just as they did, Bruno
and Rocco came tumbling through the
ivy and knocked them both down again.

'Ouch! Watch it!' said Bruno crossly,
as Rocco's foot ended up in his ear.

A moment later Granddad came striding
through the doorway, Dottie bouncing along
behind him. As soon as he saw the ivy, he
stopped dead in his tracks. The gang all
watched as he walked around the room,
laying his hand against the ivy-covered walls.

'What happened here?' he whispered.

Granddad walked out into the entrance
hall. He stopped and stared around him
as if seeing the house for the first time. A
jungle of wild ivy surrounded him, creeping
its way over the floor and up the walls and
across the ceiling. Every window, every door,

every cupboard and piece of furniture was wrapped tightly in leaves.

'I remember there being SOME ivy before, when I left,' Granddad whispered, 'but it was mostly over the wall where the doorway is. Now it's … it's everywhere!'

Jack and the gang got up and dusted themselves down, and followed Granddad into the hallway. Jack couldn't help smiling as he watched Granddad reach down and pick a fresh yellow buttercup from the moss-covered stairs. He pressed it softly against his nose.

'Beautiful!' he said. 'Well, it's grown a lot more since the last time I was here … but I must say, I rather like it!'

Just as he was saying this, a long slithering lock of ivy began prodding Rocco in the stomach as if it was sniffing at something under his top.

'Hey, cut it out!' Rocco cried, slapping

it away. 'Er … guys? The ivy's doing that magical stuff again!'

'Oh don't worry,' said Granddad. 'It won't do you any harm. It just wants to play with you, that's all.'

'Stop it, I don't want to play!' Rocco shouted. He turned away from the ivy, as if shielding something from it, and as he did so, something fell out of his top and landed with a heavy thud on the floor.

No one could believe their eyes.

There on the floor was a giant egg, the one Dottie had discovered in the bushes. It now sat slowly spinning to a stop in the middle of the room. The gang all stared at the egg, and then at Rocco, waiting for him to explain himself.

'I … I thought it would be a nice souvenir,' Rocco said with a cheeky shrug. 'It's just a little egg.'

'Just a little egg?' Bruno gasped.

But before Rocco could answer, there was a loud cracking sound. Everyone jumped back as the egg spilt open and … a baby bird hopped out.

At first, Jack couldn't figure out what it was. He thought baby chicks were supposed to be small. This baby chick wasn't small at all. It was large and fluffy. Its little wings and feet were tiny compared to the rest of its body and its curved beak seemed too large for its face. Its big bulging eyes seemed to settle on Rocco and they blinked up at him with great affection.

'Squawk!' it said.

'What's it saying?' Rocco asked Jack and Blossom excitedly.

'It just squawked,' said Jack.

'Perhaps it doesn't know how to talk yet?' said Blossom. 'It has only just been born.'

'Squawk!' said the bird again, waddling

over to Rocco.

'I think he likes you, Rocco!' said Jack. 'He probably thinks you're his mum.'

'What is he? He looks so funny!' Blossom chuckled as she crawled on her belly towards it.

Dottie came forward too and sniffed at the bird curiously.

'What is it, a pigeon?' Rocco asked.

'A pigeon!?' Bruno blurted. 'Even *fully grown* pigeons don't get as big as that!'

Jack looked over at his granddad, whose jaw Jack realised had almost dropped to the floor.

'Oh my golly goodness,' Granddad whispered.

'What?' said Blossom. 'What is it?'

'It's a dodo …' Granddad muttered.

'It can't be,' said Jack.

'Aren't they supposed to be extinct?' asked Rocco.

'Yes …' said Granddad a little breathlessly. 'Yes, they are supposed to be very extinct. Since 1681 …'

'That's ages ago …' said Bruno.

Jack could see his granddad was completely dumbfounded by this astounding discovery. He had never seen his sparkling eyes so wide before. It looked as if he was about to burst. And then he did!

'Yaaahh-hoooooo!' he roared with delight, leaping into the air as he did so.

'Isn't he something?' Granddad marvelled, dancing up and down. 'Do you realise what this means? It means everything! It means the other world is … is a paradise! A heaven for all creatures, whether old or young or even extinct … they can flourish there! They can live for ever! There must be all sorts of long-forgotten creatures out there. There could be woolly mammoths or sabre-toothed tigers or …'

'Dinosaurs!' cried Rocco excitedly.

'Let's be grateful we've got a dodo on our hands then and not a T. rex …' said Bruno, who was looking a little freaked out by this point.

'Well!' said Granddad as he began heading up the moss-covered stairs. 'This makes my mission here even more important. We need to get moving! There's so much to do and we don't have much time …'

'Wait!' Jack cried out. 'I've got to get back home to my dad! He's going to be worried sick!'

Granddad stopped still on the stairs.

'Oh no, Mum and Dad!' said Rocco. 'I completely forgot … we ran off and left them in the middle of the storm!'

'Ah yes, your parents,' said Granddad

with a small huff, 'I forgot you had those.'

'Jack's right,' Bruno said. 'We need to get back home.'

'Yeah, and I'm starving as well! I haven't eaten in ages!' said Rocco.

Granddad thought for a second and then hurried over to one of the windows. He opened it as wide as it would go and stuck his head out into the rain.

'Well!' he shouted back to them cheerfully as ever. 'Another day shouldn't hold us back too much! It doesn't look like this storm is in a hurry to disappear anytime soon.' He then slammed the window shut again. 'Let's meet back here tomorrow!'

'Come on, Dottie,' Bruno called out. 'Let's get you home.'

'What do we do with this little guy?' said Jack pointing to the fluffy dodo standing in the middle of the room.

'He can come with me!' said Rocco,

scooping him up protectively. '*I* found him.'

'Yeah right,' Bruno scoffed. 'Like Mum and Dad won't freak out when they see that thing fall out of your top on to the kitchen table!'

'Maybe it's best if the dodo stays here for now,' said Granddad, putting his arms out. 'You can have him back in the morning.'

Rocco made to pass the baby dodo to Granddad, but as he did so the bird let out a teeny squawk of distress.

'That's so cute!' said Blossom. 'He doesn't want to leave Rocco!'

Granddad let out a small chuckle and said, 'Perhaps then, young Rocco, he should stay with you.'

'Really?' said

Rocco. 'Oh thank you!'

'Oh great,' Bruno sighed. 'Mum's gonna have a fit if she finds out.'

'Well, make sure she doesn't then!' said Granddad, giving the bird a little stroke goodbye. 'And be gentle with the little tyke. He's still only a baby, don't forget.'

'He'll be safe with me,' said Rocco softly and rubbed the little bird's head with his hand.

'Excellent! Well, see you in the morning, boys!' said Granddad. 'I want to see you bright and early! We've already wasted such precious time as it is! We have a lot of plans to make, so once you have slept and dreamt the night away you must hurry back here as quick as you can! Now go on! Get out of here! Beat it! Scram! A big supper and an early night for all of you, please! You're going to need your strength tomorrow!'

FATHER AND SON

The noises from the storm had quietened as Jack sprinted all the way home. He ran as fast as he could, down the stairs and out of the front door of the old house, through the dark ivy tunnel that led to the gate, through the gate and into the alley behind his house.

He should have been exhausted by now but he wasn't. The night air was cool and a sense of fear was kicking away inside his stomach as he opened his back gate and went running like crazy across the wet lawn towards his back door. All he could think about was how angry his dad was going to be with him. The last time Jack had seen him was when Jack had been caught sneaking into the animal home and his dad had brought him home again, only for Jack to leap out of the car and go running off again into the storm. Jack hadn't had any choice – he had had to go after Blossom. But he realised now how worried his dad must have been this whole time.

The house seemed very quiet as Jack pulled open the back door. All Jack could hear was the radio that had been left on in the kitchen. There was a woman's crackling voice reporting on the big storm:

"More THUNDERSTORMS and HEAVY RAIN are forecast to hit tomorrow. Storm Brian is set to bring further downpours and lightning storms are expected across the whole country by tomorrow evening. It is a stark change from the sunny skies of last week and flood warnings have now been issued.

A month's worth of rain is expected to fall in one night, the most in six years …"

Granddad was right, Jack said to himself, it didn't seem like the storm was going anywhere in a hurry. Jack gently closed the back door behind him. At first there didn't seem to be anybody home, but when Jack switched the kitchen light on there was his father. He was sitting at the table with a look of grave disappointment on his face. It looked as though he had been waiting there for a very long time.

'W-why are you sitting in the dark?' asked Jack.

Mr Broom looked up as if in surprise. 'I didn't notice it had got dark,' he said. 'I made you your tea.'

Mr Broom was still wearing his dusty overalls from work and drinking tea out of a mug he had balanced on his knee. There was a jam sandwich on a plate to the side of

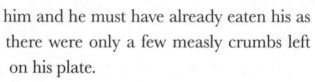

him and he must have already eaten his as there were only a few measly crumbs left on his plate.

'We never eat at the table,' said Jack.

'Well, I thought it was time for a change,' Mr Broom said. He moved the chair out from next to him and patted it.

Jack came in and sat down.

'Where have you been?' asked Mr Broom calmly. 'Have you any idea how worried I've been? You run off in the middle of a storm, I don't know where you've gone or when you'll be coming back. Anything could have happened to you.'

Jack bit his lip and stayed silent. He wanted to tell him the truth. If only he could tell his dad about everything that had happened. Jack wished it more than anything, but he just knew his dad wouldn't believe him. And he couldn't risk being grounded and not being able to go to the house tomorrow.

'I'm sorry, Dad,' said Jack, unsure what else he could say.

Mr Broom then sighed and said, 'Eat some food, you must be hungry.'

Jack began tucking into his sandwich and Mr Broom leaned back in his chair and stared out the window. Beads of rain came dribbling down the glass like racing tadpoles as silent flashes of lightning lit up the whole street outside.

'Maybe what happened today was a good thing,' Mr Broom said quietly. 'Perhaps it's time I left the animal home and tried something new.'

Jack winced as he remembered how he'd got his dad in trouble with his horrible boss, Mr Nettles. He didn't want to be the cause of him losing his job.

'I thought you loved working at the animal home?' said Jack, eating his sandwich hungrily, and licking the sticky jam from his lips.

'I love the animals, yes,' said Mr Broom, 'And when I took over from your granddad, I was so happy. I love taking care of the animals and being outdoors all day. But Mr Nettles is so horrible, and I do feel sad for the creatures sometimes ...' These words seem to come out as though Mr Broom was talking to himself.

'But you always said they were old and needed looking after,' said Jack.

'They do,' said Mr Broom. 'I just wish there was another way.'

His dad sighed deeply.

'Your mum would know what to do if she was here,' he said. 'I used to love that about her. She always had a particular talent for knowing what the right thing to do was.'

A warm and pleasant feeling swirled around inside Jack's stomach. 'I like that she's like that,' he said.

Mr Broom glanced at Jack for second

as though he might have misheard him. 'Anyway,' he said, leaning forward, 'I guess what I am trying to say is that I'm sorry I've had to work so hard and haven't been there for you, Jack.'

'You have been there for me, Dad.'

'No, I haven't,' Mr Broom interrupted. 'Not of late. I should be around more. I should be watching you grow up. It's happening so fast. I'm missing it.'

Jack watched his dad for a few more moments, not knowing what to think or what to say. Then Mr Broom suddenly clicked his fingers as though a marvellous idea had hit him. 'Why don't we hang out together tomorrow?' he said with a spark in his voice. 'Just the two of us! We'll get up bright and early and go anywhere you like, what do you say?'

'I can't,' said Jack rather abruptly. He wracked his brain for an excuse. 'I mean,

I want to, I really want to, it's just that I promised Rocco and Bruno I would help them with their … homework.'

'Their homework?' Mr Broom said, scratching his head. 'It's a bit early to be doing all that isn't it? The holidays have only just started.'

'I know but they are very behind,' said Jack very seriously. 'And I promised.'

'Well, a promise is a promise I suppose.' said Mr Broom.

Jack couldn't bear the disappointment in his father's eyes. He hated lying to him and the last thing he wanted to do was let his father down, but he had no other choice. He had to be back at the old empty house in the morning. There was no way he could let the gang down.

Mr Broom rose slowly out of his chair and began clearing the plates from the table. 'Perhaps

I should go into work tomorrow then and straighten things out with Mr Nettles,' he said, sounding a little deflated.

Jack watched him for a few moments. He felt terrible for upsetting his dad like this. 'I'm sorry I ran off, Dad,' he said. 'It won't happen again.'

'It's OK, son,' said Mr Broom, turning back to him as he reached the door. 'I'm just glad you're all right. Hey, let's have a proper dinner tomorrow night, OK? Just you and me. No excuses.'

'Sure, Dad, that would be nice,' said Jack with a smile, and his father seemed to brighten.

Jack had no idea what tomorrow night might hold in store, but he had to keep his father happy for now. Tomorrow would be a big day. As soon as Mr Broom

had left the room, Jack ran straight upstairs
to bed.

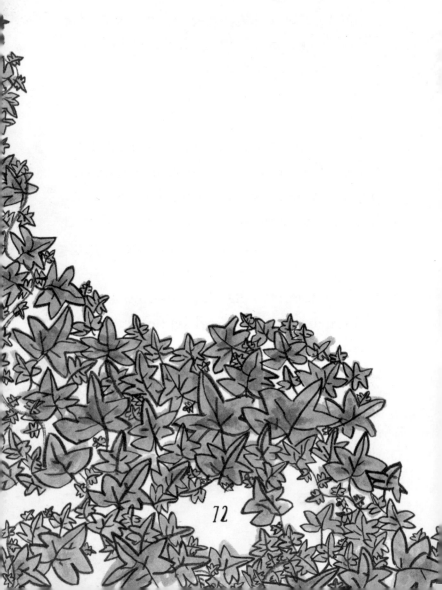

POWER SHOW!

Jack woke to the sound of tapping against his window. *It must be the rain,* he thought as he sat up slowly, rubbing the sleep from his eyes. Ozzie the cat was lying on the end of his bed, snoring away without a care in the world.

The tapping on the window seemed to be getting louder and louder, but when Jack opened his curtains to look, he found to his surprise it wasn't the rain at all. It was Blossom, perched on the windowledge tapping against the glass with her finger. She looked as happy as he had ever seen her and was grinning from ear to ear.

'What are you doing here?' asked Jack as he opened the window and let Blossom in. The rain hadn't actually started yet, but Jack could see that a blanket of thick rolling clouds had filled the whole sky.

'Morning, kid!' said Blossom with an excited whisper.

'What time is it?' asked Jack with a big yawn.

'It's time you got dressed, you lazy bear!' she said. 'Come on, hurry up!'

Ozzie twitched his long white whiskers and with his eyes still closed he meowed, 'Will someone please shut her up.'

'I heard that,' said Blossom, glaring at the old cat with narrowing eyes.

'Don't mind him,' said Jack with his hair pointing up in every direction. 'He's a bit of an old grouch in the mornings.'

'How dare you,' mumbled Ozzie, rolling over and going back to sleep.

Jack looked at the clock – it was half past nine already. He had meant to be there by now. He began bouncing around the room, dressing as quickly as he could. It suddenly occurred to him that this was the first time he and Blossom had been alone together since he'd discovered who she really was. He couldn't quite believe that the girl standing in front of him was – or used to be – his mum. The whole bizarre and ludicrous truth was right there resting on the tip of his tongue and a voice in Jack's head was urging him to say something, to tell her the truth. But how could he? She was just a kid herself. As Granddad had said – she just wouldn't understand. And their friendship would be ruined. No, Jack told himself, he would have to keep his secret for now and leave it to his granddad to sort out this magical mess.

There was really no other way. He would try and talk to him again at some point today.

Blossom clicked her fingers right in front of Jack's nose. 'Stop day-dreaming, kid!' she said. 'We need to hurry! Come on, grab your coat!'

'I have to say goodbye to my dad,' said Jack, grabbing his jacket and ushering Blossom back out of the window. 'I'll meet you in the alley.'

'OK, but be quick!' said Blossom as she went sliding down the drainpipe.

Jack quickly said goodbye to his dad through the gap in his door and ran downstairs. He grabbed his trainers and pulled them on as he hopped out of the back door and through the gate at the bottom of his garden that led to the alley.

Blossom, Bruno and Rocco stood waiting by the gate to the old house. Bruno and Rocco were both yawning their heads off, and Dottie was there too, wagging her tail happily. She barked a good morning to Jack as he arrived, panting, in front of them.

'Morning, Dottie!' said Jack and gave her a scratch behind the ears.

'She broke in!' said Bruno, pointing at Blossom, clearly outraged. 'Blossom actually broke into our house, climbed on to my bed and woke me up by whacking a pillow over my head!'

'At least she didn't just drag you out of bed by your feet!' Rocco grumbled, rubbing his sore backside. 'I bruise like a peach!'

'Oh come on, you big babies!' Blossom shouted as she went sprinting through the gate of the old empty house, with Dottie tearing after her, barking excitedly.

Jack and the Buckleys followed behind. Jack looked around in wonder as he climbed the narrow staircase. The house looked the same as it always did, but the pure sight of it still took Jack's breath away – the magical ivy rising and twisting its way up the staircase and across the ceiling, the curling vines covering almost every inch of wall. It was the most wondrous sight to behold.

'Where is he then?' asked Rocco when they got to the top.

'Where's who?' said Blossom.

'Your dad!' said Bruno. 'You haven't lost him again, have you?'

'Oh yeah!' Blossom cried. 'I forgot for a second … he's this way!'

'You and your memory …' Bruno sighed, shaking his head as they followed Blossom through the entrance hall and up the central stairs, into the room above that always seemed to Jack to be slanting to one side.

Blossom's tent where the gang had first found her was still resting peacefully in one corner of the room, while in the other corner steam was rising from the cooking pot hanging over the wood-burning stove. Granddad was sitting next to it on the floor and sharing hot milk from an old gravy jug with Dottie, who had got there before them.

'One slurp for you and one slurp for me!' Granddad chuckled.

'This is the best milk I've ever tasted!' barked Dottie.

'Well, the absolute key is the temperature!' Granddad told her. 'Milk's got to be either freezing cold or cosy warm, that's what I say! Anything in between and I can't stomach the stuff! I just spit it out!'

'They're all here, Dad!' Blossom cried. 'I had to drag them out of bed!'

Granddad leapt up off the floor and spread his arms out wide to them. 'Welcome, my little friends!' he cried. 'I hope you all got enough sleep! We've got a big day ahead! Now, Blossom, pass me that spare bowl please,' he said, filling it up with milk and handing it to the others.

Everyone took turns in taking a warm swig. When the bowl came to Rocco, he unzipped his coat and the baby dodo's head popped out.

'So that's where you've been hiding him!' Granddad chuckled.

'Terry will love a bit of milk for his breakfast,' said Rocco.

'Terry!?' Bruno scoffed. 'You've named him?'

'Yep!' Rocco said proudly as he dipped his finger into the bowl and let little droplets of milk fall off it into the baby bird's beak.

'Squawk!' said Terry happily.

'You can't call a bird Terry!' cried Bruno.

'Why can't I?' Rocco protested 'I like the name Terry! It

suits him.'

'I think Terry's a great name!' agreed Blossom. 'I couldn't have picked a better one myself!'

'I agree. Terry's a fine name for a young dodo!' said Granddad. 'So we're all here! How splendid! Now, young Jack here mentioned to me yesterday that you all have powers? Which one of you is as fast as a cheetah?'

'That would be me,' said Bruno, puffing out his chest.

There was a short pause before Granddad looked him up and down and said, 'Well? Show us what you've got then.'

Bruno suddenly exploded forward and went whizzing around the room with a streak of light trailing out behind him. He went round and round and round and then came to a skidding stop. The speed had made all of Bruno's hair stick up on end as if he had been given an electric shock and when Jack glanced down, he noticed smoke coming off the soles of Bruno's trainers.

'Mightily impressive!' cried Granddad. 'That was amazing! You could win every gold medal at the Olympics with that power up your sleeve! It looks like a lot of fun too!'

'It's the best thing ever!' Bruno panted, catching his breath.

'I've never actually tried that particular one myself,' said Granddad, 'but I'm glad it works so well! Glorious stuff! Absolutely marvellous!'

Bruno smiled smugly round at everyone. Blossom gave him a big thumbs up before grabbing hold of Rocco and pushing him forward.

'So YOU must be the boy who can fly?' said Granddad, looking down at Rocco. 'I attempted it a few times myself, but I could never seem to get the hang of it. Every time

I shot up into the air I would always come tumbling back down again. There was one time I ended up in a neighbour's garden. He never looked at me the same after that and I've never flown again since! I'm getting too old for all that flying around stuff now anyway. Flying's a young man's game! So, come on then, young Rocco, give us a show!'

Rocco placed Terry gently on to the floor, clenched his little fists and went shooting up into the air, all the way to the ceiling, where he circled around an old chandelier which was wrapped tight in leaves.

'He's really got the hang of it, hasn't he?' said Granddad, giggling as Rocco came swooping back down over their heads like a low-flying bird, before landing back on the floor again. He smiled round at everyone, showing all of his front teeth. The gang all clapped and cheered and Dottie let out a big old howl.

'You're a talented bunch!' said Granddad, raising his voice above the noise. 'And these talents of yours will come in handy when I tell you about my mission!'

'What about mine and Jack's talents?' said Blossom, sounding a little jealous.

'Those will be especially important!' said Granddad.

'What is the mission, Dad? Tell us!' said Blossom eagerly.

Jack was watching his granddad intently. 'When we were in the other world, you said you made a promise to an old friend ...' Jack prompted.

'Indeed I did,' said Granddad.

'Which friend?' cried Blossom.

'Jumbo,' said Granddad.

'Jumbo the elephant? From the animal home?' asked Blossom, her eyes growing huge.

'The very same. I'm going to take him with me,' said Granddad. 'I'm going to take ALL of them with me.'

'All of who?' asked Bruno, sounding confused. 'Who are you taking with you?'

'The animals,' said Granddad. 'All of the animals from the animal home. We're going to break them all out and I'm going to take them back with me into the other world.'

GRANDDAD'S PLAN

Granddad stared at the little gang that stood before him and the gang stared straight back at him. Bruno then snorted and they all started giggling.

'That was a good one!' Rocco chuckled. 'You had us there for a second!'

After a few moments the laughing stopped. That's when Jack noticed that Granddad's face hadn't changed.

'You're not being serious?' Jack said.

'I am being completely serious,' Granddad replied defiantly. 'I made a promise to Jumbo that I was going to come back and take him

87

with me. I've never broken a promise. Not ever!'

'We're taking Jumbo with us!?' cried Blossom excitedly. 'That's a fantastic idea!'

Jack felt a sudden twist of panic inside his stomach. Blossom seemed so excited at the idea of leaving for the other world. Jack couldn't bear to lose her again. Without thinking he blurted out, 'You can't! You can't go!'

There was a short silence as everyone turned to look at him.

'I mean, you can't *do that*!' said Jack, covering quickly. 'You can't just take Jumbo and all the animals with you!'

'Why can't I?' said Granddad.

'Because it's a crazy idea!' Bruno cried. 'We'll get caught! There'll be security cameras!'

'Then we'll just have to find a way to switch them off, won't we,' said Granddad determinedly.

'And how do we get all the animals out?' asked Rocco. 'The cages are all locked.'

'That's easy,' said Granddad. 'We steal Jack's dad's keys.'

'What?' said Jack.

'Perfect!' said Blossom.

'Now,' said Granddad, clapping his huge hands together with a loud bang, as if that was settled, 'is everyone ready?'

'Yeah!' said Blossom, leaping into the air. Rocco and Bruno were looking excited now too. It was only Jack who was staring around him as if in shock.

'Wonderful!' cried Granddad. 'Now follow me!'

Granddad scuttled out of the room and headed down the stairs with his big heavy boots going *boof boof boof* all the way.

The gang followed after him as he headed into the little room to the left at the bottom of the staircase. Granddad went bursting through the door. Inside the room there was the bedroom Jack had discovered when he'd first explored the house, with its four-poster bed and the little en suite bathroom, with its bed, bath and toilet all completely overgrown with ivy.

'Did this used to be your bed?' asked Rocco as he gazed at all the ivy twisting itself around the mattress and curling its way up the pillars.

'What do you mean, did it *used* to be?' said Granddad. 'It still is! I slept on it last night!'

'You slept on that bed last night?' cried Bruno.

'Yes, why not? What's wrong with it?' asked Granddad.

'It's covered in all those leaves and vines!' said Bruno. 'You could get your neck wrapped up in all that and then you'd be sorry.'

'Oh the ivy will never hurt you!' said Granddad, still roaming around the room as though he had misplaced something. 'It will never hurt anyone. Nature such as this is too healing and kind. It would rather play with you more than anything else! Besides, it can always hear you.'

'Hear you?' said Rocco with a frown.

'Oh yes,' said Granddad. 'It can even do as it's told on occasion.'

'Show us, Dad, please!' begged Blossom.

Granddad gave a small huff as though he were being interrupted by something very unimportant. 'Dear, dear, dear,' he sighed, shaking his head. 'We really don't have time for this, but if you insist on stalling the proceedings with all these questions, I suppose I have no other choice!'

He then clapped his hands together three

times and all at once, the ivy began to magically unwrap itself from the mattress and slide away from the bed.

Dottie, who had followed them into the room, now scrambled backwards out of it again as the magical ivy obediently pulled back to reveal a perfectly comfy-looking bed.

'You see!' cried Granddad. 'Doesn't look half as bad now, does it? Now where is it …' muttered Granddad, who seemed to be looking under one of the pillows for something.

'Ah-ha!' he cried. 'Here it is!'

In his hand he held up a gold key.

'Now come on!' Granddad said as he moved on through to the little bathroom.

Jack couldn't help wondering why on earth they were heading into the bathroom. They all crowded into the tiny room behind Granddad. The room was so small that it

could barely fit all of them inside.

'What are we supposed to do in here?' whispered Bruno to the others.

Granddad climbed up and stood on top of the toilet.

'I wonder if this still works?' he said, and pulled down hard on the dangling chain next to his head. The gang all waited excitedly, wondering what was going to happen.

Nothing happened at first, then there came a huge flushing noise as loud as a crashing wave.

'Well, at least the plumbing still works!' cried Granddad joyously.

'We haven't just come in here to watch you flush the toilet, have we?' asked Rocco.

'Far from it!' said Granddad, leaping off the toilet and crouching down on the floor. Once more, he seemed to be looking for something.

Dottie was sniffing the floor there too.

'There's something under here ...' Dottie barked.

'Indeed there is, you clever dog!' said Granddad, as he slid the key into a tiny hole in the floor and, with a twist and a lift, pulled open a hatch.

The gang all peered over his shoulder excitedly.

'It's a trapdoor!' cried Rocco.

'It's a secret passageway!' said Jack, suddenly realising what he was looking at.

'No way!' Blossom cried.

'It looks dark down there ...' said Bruno peering down anxiously.

'Of course it looks dark down there!' said Granddad, slapping him on the back.

'It's underground! Ah, but just you wait until you see what's inside! Let's go!'

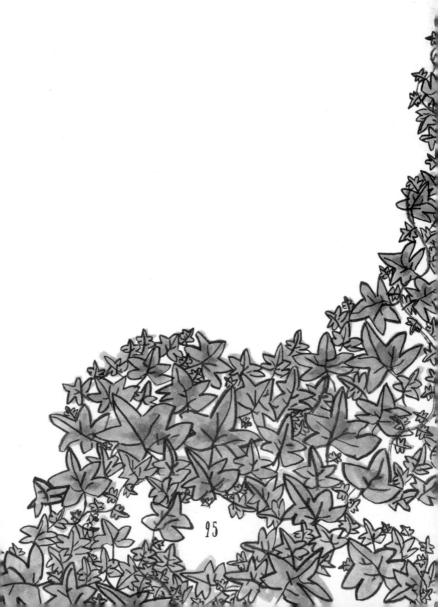

THE MAP

Jack knew he should be worried about Blossom going back to the other world, about his granddad's ridiculous plans, about having to steal his dad's keys and break all the animals out of the animal home. But right now as he stepped down the ladder into the darkness below, he had to admit he felt a thrill of excitement.

'Our very own underground hideout!' Blossom whispered into Jack's ear.

'It's a secret part to the house,' said Granddad as he made his way down the ladder. 'Nobody's ever been down here

97

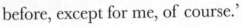

before, except for me, of course.'

'Don't forget me!' barked Dottie, who was stuck at the top, looking down at them all through the hatch.

'Come here, Dottie' said Bruno, reaching up to lift her down.

'I didn't even know this was here!' said Blossom.

'You'll find there are many undiscovered things inside this house,' said Granddad, and he winked at Jack with those sparkling eyes of his. Jack could feel sharp nervous tingles in his tummy that shot all the way down to his toes as he stared around the dark underground passageway. To the right he spotted a door. 'What's behind that?' he asked Granddad.

'Many mysterious and beautiful things,' said Granddad, walking towards it. He opened the door and a colourful blaze of light lit up the whole underground space.

'Come along then,' he said, 'we haven't got all day,' and he ushered the gang inside.

'What is this place?' asked Rocco. Terry's little head was popping out of his coat and he gave it a comforting stroke.

'It looks like a magical cave,' said Blossom.

Jack could see one of the walls was lined with shelves and on the shelves there were rows and rows of little glass bottles, filled with sparkling lights.

'They look just like the bottles we got our powers from!' said Bruno. 'I thought there weren't any left.'

'It's true, most of the ones I had in the house upstairs were smashed in the great storm,' said Granddad, 'and their spilling of course was what created the magical ivy, and the doorway. Luckily I still had a few stashed away safely down here!'

'They're so beautiful.' Blossom said, staring around admiringly. 'Are there gobstoppers inside like the ones we found?'

'This one's got some weird misty stuff inside,' said Rocco, inspecting one of the bottles on his tiptoes.

Inside the bottle there seemed to be some kind of bright burning gas. It looked like sparkling flakes of reddish-green smoke.

'Some of them are solid spheres, some liquid, others just a mist-like scent,' said Granddad. 'It depends on the animal the magic comes from.'

'Can we have one?' asked Bruno.

'All in good time,' said Granddad, taking off his long dark coat and laying it on the table next to him. 'First come and have a look at this.' He hurried over to the far end of the room where some sort of large poster had been pinned to the wall.

'I was up half the night planning this!' said Granddad excitedly. 'I had to draw it from memory, but I think it's pretty accurate!' He switched on a small light that was hanging above the poster.

'It's a map!' cried Rocco.

'Yes, but not just any map!' said Granddad.

Jack leaned in closely and could see lots of little pathways and square shaped blocks with animal names written on them. 'It's a map of the animal home,' said Jack.

'You've got it in one, Jack!' said Granddad. 'It's a map of the animal home in its entirety. I know every nook and cranny of that place! I know it better than the back of my own hand!' Granddad was becoming very excited now. Jack could almost see all the little cogs turning inside his mind as he began forming a plan. 'First, we need to know when the storm will be over.'

'The storm will be over by morning,' said Jack. 'I heard it on the radio last night.'

'Well, that's settled then,' Granddad said.

'We break the animals out tonight!'

'We're doing this *tonight*?' Jack blurted out.

'Of course tonight!' his granddad cried, hopping wildly into the air. 'The storm will be over by morning and when the storm stops, the doorway will close!' he said, grabbing a long stick of bamboo from the side and waving it around emphatically. 'So,' he went on, pacing restlessly in front of his map, 'the plan is this! We'll arrive at midnight, so you three boys will all have to figure out a way to sneak out of your homes without your parents knowing.'

'Oh, we're used to that,' said Bruno breezily.

'That's perfect then!' said Granddad cheerfully, and he flicked the stick of bamboo against Jack's chest. 'Jack, you'll have to steal your father's keys before you go to bed and bring them with you when you come.'

Jack didn't feel good about this idea at all,

but decided now wasn't the moment to say anything.

'And don't worry,' his granddad said, 'we're only borrowing them. He'll get them right back.'

'Yes, but they won't be much use to him once the animals have all been freed!' said Jack.

'Well, let's cross that bridge when we come to it,' said Granddad, who was clearly ready to move on to the next part of the plan. 'Now, once we're inside, I'll cut the power, which will knock out the security cameras.'

Jack couldn't believe what he was hearing, but he could see Blossom, Bruno and Rocco were nodding along with Granddad's every word.

'Jack and Blossom, you'll have the keys to the central area

of the animal home,' said Granddad, and he slapped the stick with a whack in the middle of the map. 'This is where most of the animals are. You'll start with the birds – owls, storks, flamingos, that sort of thing – and then you'll work your way round the monkey enclosure to the farm animals over here – donkeys, chickens, ducks, pigs. Don't let the smell bother you and don't let those mouthy geese give you any trouble. With the gift of language you both possess, you'll be able to show them who's boss right away!'

Jack turned to Blossom nervously but she didn't seem anxious in the slightest and was watching the whole presentation with a look of wonder in her eyes.

'Now, Bruno,' Granddad went on, 'you'll have the keys to the outer rim. The enclosures are spaced out more here for the animals to roam – giraffes, zebras, kangaroos. You'll need to cover more ground and with that keen speed of yours, you'll be able to get every one of those enclosures open quicker than lightning!'

The gang could see that Granddad was getting more and more excited as the plan was coming together.

'Once the animals are out of their enclosures, your next job will be to help steer them towards the main gate – which might not be as easy as it sounds! Rocco, my dear lad – you'll be able to help with this. You will be our watchful eye in the sky! You can guide us and be our lookout, let us know if any of the animals are hiding or sleeping, or if we have any unwanted human visitors.'

'Can Terry come too?' said Rocco.

'Of course he can!' cried Granddad. 'Dodos can't fly though, so you'll have to keep him tucked up safely inside your jacket. Oh, and speaking of jackets – I hope you've all got waterproofs at home, as we might be in for a bit of rain tonight!'

'What will you do, Dad?' asked Blossom.

'I will take care of my dear friend Jumbo! And then together we'll come and help usher all the animals through the main gate and into the car park, here.' Once again, he slapped the stick hard against the map with a terrific thwack. 'Then all we need to do is get the animals to follow us from there back up the hill!'

Blossom suddenly leapt into the air with a whispered cry of joy. 'This is going to be so much fun!' she cried. 'It's just what the secret summer gang was made for! Can you imagine how happy the animals will be?'

Jack didn't say anything. He was just staring

at his granddad now. He couldn't believe that this wacky old man actually thought they could break into an animal home and release every animal inside it without getting caught. Even if they managed to get them all out, how on earth were they going to bring them back to the doorway? What were they going to do? Walk them all the way back through the middle of the town? Never mind the fact they would be putting his dad out of a job. It was an impossible idea! It was ludicrous! And at the end of it, was Blossom then going to breeze off into the other world and out of Jack's life for ever? All these thoughts and questions were rolling around inside Jack's head like clothes in a tumble dryer.

'What's wrong, lad?' asked Granddad, who was now staring back at him.

Jack felt like he was stuck between two hard rocks. His head had gone all squidgy as though his brain had started melting. He didn't know what to say.

'You do want to help, don't you?' Blossom said to him, a hurt tone creeping into her voice.

'Of course I do,' said Jack, taking a moment before he spoke again. 'It's just … my dad would never forgive me,' he said quietly. 'He'll have nowhere to work if there are no animals at the home any more. We'd be taking away his job.'

'I gave him that job,' said Granddad dismissively. 'I'm sure he won't mind me taking it back!'

'You gave him his job?' asked Blossom, confused. 'I didn't know you even knew him.'

Granddad had an expression on his face like he'd just swallowed a bug. 'Well, I mean … ummm,' he stuttered, 'not literally, but, you know …' he said, waving his stick vaguely in the air. 'Anyway, there are far better jobs out there he could be getting on with. He'll soon be getting over it. Perhaps he'll become a great sailor or maybe your dad can get a job in one of those sweet factories and spend all day testing the jellies and gumballs! That's the job I always wanted to have!'

'That sounds like the best job ever!' Rocco cried.

'Yeah but you'd be fired on your first day for eating them all,' said Bruno.

Everyone was now laughing. Everyone that is except for Jack, who was staring at the ground. Blossom put her arm around him and rested her head upon his shoulder. Jack's throat went all tight with all the things he couldn't say to her and for one horrible moment, he thought he might cry.

The truth was, he just didn't want her to go, and he didn't know if he could trust Granddad not to take her with him. She was

Granddad's daughter after all, just as much as she was Jack's mum.

There was quite a long silence and Jack was trying to work out what to say, when Granddad knelt down in front of him. He watched Jack for a few moments and when he spoke again, it was in a soft and quiet voice. 'Tell me, Jack,' he said, 'do you think all those animals should be locked away inside that place?'

'Well, no, but it's a home for old animals, isn't it? Animals that need looking after?' said Jack.

'Don't you think that they could be better looked after without gates and cages?'

After a short pause, Jack nodded.

'I think so too …' his Granddad said softly. 'It took me a long time to realise that. But you know what? I think deep down your father feels the same way.'

'He did say it made him sad sometimes …'

said Jack.

'There you are then!' his granddad said.

Jack looked up into his granddad's eyes. The whole of his face was filled with warmth and adventure.

'What do you say, young Jack? Shall we go and set them free?'

Jack turned to Blossom, remembering what his dad had said the other night – that his mum had always known what the right thing to do was. 'Do you think this is the right thing to do?' he asked, looking straight into her big green eyes.

'I do,' she said, looking back at him with absolute certainty.

Jack sighed. 'OK, fine …' he said, a smile playing at the corner of his mouth. 'Let's do it.'

Blossom jumped up with a twirl through the air and kissed Jack on the head. 'Oh thank you thank you thank you!'

'But how are we going to get all the animals to follow us back here?' said Jack.

'Well I'm glad you asked!' said Granddad as he picked his coat up and put it back on. 'That is my next genius part of the plan! Come on, you lot! It's time we headed on through the passageway!'

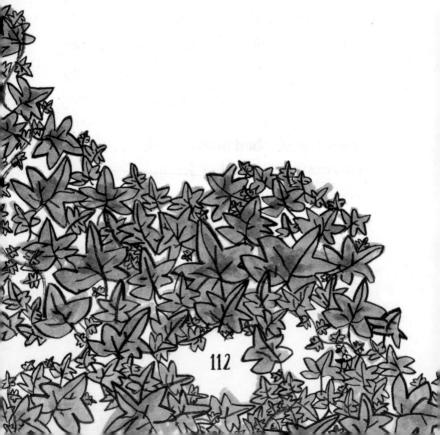

THE SECRET
ORCHARD

'We must hurry!' Granddad called out as he led them out of the magical cave and down to the end of the passageway. 'Link hands and keep close together. You don't want anyone getting lost down here. That could be disastrous!'

Blossom grabbed hold of Jack's hand and Rocco grabbed a hold of Bruno's.

'Hold someone else's hand, you weirdo!' said Bruno, slapping it away.

Terry let out an angry squawk and glared at Bruno with little frowning eyes.

'Did you see that?' Blossom chuckled.

'Terry's defending you, Rocco. He thinks you're his mum!'

A proud smile flashed across Rocco's face. 'Ah, wicked!' he said.

'There you go, Rocco,' Bruno scoffed, 'you can start wearing all mum's clothes now.'

Rocco ignored his brother. 'You're just jealous YOU don't have a baby dodo to look up to YOU!' he said, then walked on down the corridor, muttering things into Terry's ear like, 'Don't listen to him, Terry!' and 'You're gonna be safe with me!'

'Come along, children!' said Granddad. 'This way!'

Through the underground passageway they went. They were all linked together in a long chain with Granddad leading at the front. Holding tight on to Blossom's hand, Jack surged forward through the dark. The air was becoming cooler all the time as they continued hurtling through the secret passageway.

Dottie began sniffing at the air as she bounded along and barked, 'I can smell trees and fresh grass!'

'There's a light at the end of the tunnel, look!' said Blossom, pointing ahead.

As she said it, the ground beneath them started to slope gently upwards, and soon the gang found themselves racing out of a tunnel and up into the light of day.

Jack looked around him and realised that they were in the back garden, on the other side of the house.

'Here we are at last!' Granddad announced.

The gang now found themselves standing in the middle of a great orchard surrounded by apple trees.

'I remember this place.' said Blossom.

Granddad bent down and lifted her up on to his shoulders. 'We used to pick apples here when you were little,' he said.

'Hey, I still am little!' she said, tugging his beard.

'Oh yes! Of course you are!' Granddad chuckled with a little side glance to Jack.

Jack smiled and said nothing as Bruno emerged from the tunnel and stared around him. 'It's like a secret garden.' he muttered.

'So it is,' said Granddad. 'Which is most appropriate, because now it's time for the next part of my plan …'

The gang all stared at him, waiting excitedly for the next piece in the puzzle.

'Apples!' Granddad announced.

'Apples?' said the gang in unison, their faces screwed up in confusion.

'Yes, apples!' repeated Granddad excitedly. 'We're going to collect them and take them with us tonight! If there's one thing that animals love, it's apples! It's such a wonderful treat for them! Whether they're chopped or mashed or swallowed down whole! They simply can't get over the taste! They go mad for the sweetness! I used to take barrels of them into the animal home every time I went. That was until old Grumpy Nettles took over the place! He only allowed them to have soggy old vegetables. The vicious brute!'

'I can't believe you've got a house full of magic, and apples is your best plan!' said Bruno grumpily.

'Look, there's some buckets over there we can put them in!' said Blossom.

'Yeah, but how are we going to get them all to the animal home?' asked Bruno. 'We can't lug buckets full of apples all the way down the hill, can we.'

That's when Jack noticed that Granddad was leaning up against something. At first it looked like a huge mound of compost or something, it was so overgrown with great locks of twisted ivy. Very carefully Granddad began peeling them all away, and Jack realised that beneath the ivy was a sheet, and beneath the sheet was some sort of large object.

Granddad took a deep breath and said, 'I am about to show you something so fantastically great! I'm almost scared to show you, it's so brilliant!'

The gang remained silent.

Jack could feel his hands going all tingly right through to the tips of his fingers and then like a magician, Granddad whipped the entire sheet up into the air.

The gang blinked at it.

'What is it?' asked Blossom.

'Is it a space ship?' asked Rocco excitedly.

'What do you mean, what is it?' cried Granddad. 'It's my old Beetle!'

'It's a car,' said Jack.

'It's a piece of junk!' said Bruno.

'A piece of junk!?' Granddad bellowed. 'How dare you! This is my most prized and valuable possession! I bought this car back in 1969 and she hasn't once let me down yet!'

Jack had to agree with

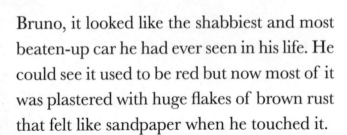

Bruno, it looked like the shabbiest and most beaten-up car he had ever seen in his life. He could see it used to be red but now most of it was plastered with huge flakes of brown rust that felt like sandpaper when he touched it.

'I thought you were going to show us a crazy invention or something magical!' cried Rocco.

'Ah, you don't get much more magical than this!' cried Granddad gleefully. 'An old classic like this is sheer magic at its best! We'll fill her up to the brim with all the apples we can! Then we'll drive it down to the animal home, and once we've freed all the animals, we'll tempt them back up the hill with the apples!'

'So, apples and a car ... that's your plan?' said Bruno.

'I think it's an excellent plan!' said Blossom. 'How many do we need?'

'All of them,' said Granddad, placing her

back on the ground.

'All of them!?' cried Bruno. 'How are we going to do that?'

'Don't tell me a talented bunch like you can't be rounding up an orchard full of apples with all the amazing powers you have?' said Granddad cheerfully. 'Judging by those clouds up there, that storm will be arriving again soon. It looks like it's going to be a big one tonight, so we'd better get cracking!'

As he said it, there was a deep rumbling sound in the distance. Jack looked anxiously up into the dark rolling clouds above.

'I've got it!' Blossom cried. 'Rocco, you fly around collecting apples from the tops of the trees and Bruno can whizz around and grab the ones at the bottom! Me and Jack can fetch the buckets and catch the ones Rocco throws down!'

'That's great, Blossom!' Granddad cried.

'Once the buckets are full, we'll tip them all into the boot of the car! Go on now, get going!'

So Jack and Blossom raced over and collected a bucket each, ready to catch all the apples. Rocco unzipped his coat and placed Terry on to the ground. 'Now you be careful, Terry,' he said. 'Don't go wandering off too far.'

'Squawk!' said Terry, looking up at him lovingly before pecking happily at the grass. Then Rocco went soaring up into the sky. A moment later, Bruno zoomed off too, and disappeared. He reappeared again in an instant with an arm full of bright green apples. Jack was so stunned by Bruno's speed that he just stood there staring at him. 'You're getting better at all this zooming around stuff, aren't you, Bruno?' Jack said to him.

'Better and faster, Jacky-boy!' said Bruno with a wicked grin. He tipped the apples into

Jack's bucket and exploded off again.

Rocco was now inside one of the apple trees, manoeuvring himself upward through the twisted branches. The spiky twigs pulled at his clothes like old witches' fingers but he didn't seem to mind. He looked like an astronaut bobbing about up there on a new mission to save the world. 'You guys ready?' he shouted down, with his arms full of apples.

'Ready!' they shouted, and a moment later a shower of apples came raining down, landing directly into Blossom's bucket.

'Nice shot, Rocco!' she cheered.

As Bruno came back with another armful, an apple from above came sailing down and hit Bruno on the head. 'Hey!' Bruno shouted, glaring up at his brother. 'That wasn't funny!'

'I thought it was!' said Rocco cheekily

before flying off again and on to the next tree.

'He's a good shot!' said Granddad. 'You see! We'll have all these apples collected up in no time! The animals will be so happy when we turn up with all these tonight! They won't know what hit them! There'll be no more horrible soggy vegetables for them whilst I'm around!'

By now, everyone was very excited. Even Dottie began collecting a few stray apples and deposited them in the boot with her tail wagging like crazy.

More and more apples came raining down all afternoon into the buckets. Jack and Blossom were dashing around and diving over one another to catch them. When the buckets were full, Jack and Blossom would tip them into the boot of the car and go rushing back for more. It had very quickly become an all-out competition of who could catch the most and when the final apple came tumbling down out of the sky, Granddad caught it with his hand and took a huge bite.

'I think that's the last one!' he said as everyone stepped away from the boot of the car, which was now stuffed full of apples.

The gang gathered round, all satisfyingly tired and out of breath.

'So that's it, is it?' said Bruno. 'A car full of apples. That's your big plan …'

There was a bright twinkle in Granddad's eyes and a clever smile played across his lips. 'Well, perhaps we could use a little something to help us …' he said, as he reached into his pocket and pulled out a small bottle.

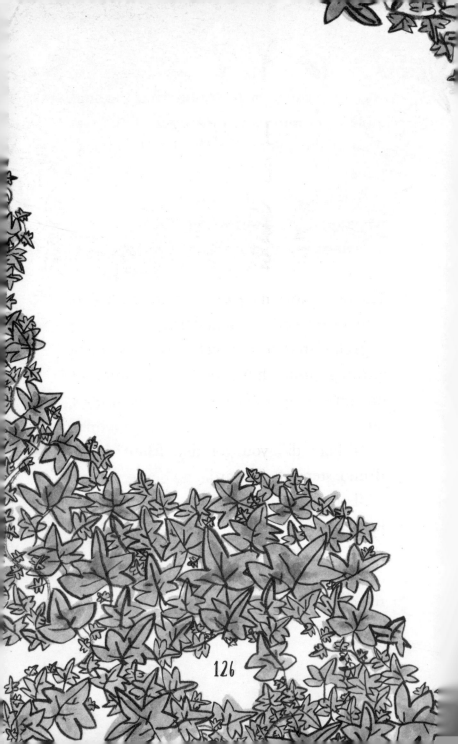

THE MAGIC BOTTLE

The bottle was made out of thick dark glass with a fresh cork stuck in the top.

Jack stared at it, a feeling of excitement growing inside him. Within the walls of the glass, a sparkly substance was swirling around.

'Where did you get that from?' asked Bruno, stepping forward.

'Is it from the cave?' Blossom whispered in surprise.

'It is indeed,' said Granddad.

'That was sneaky!' said Rocco, staring at the others.

The gang gathered round closely, as Granddad held the bottle out under their noses and a blaze of light from inside lit up the children's faces.

'Is it a gobstopper?' asked Rocco.

'Or a scent?' asked Jack, remembering what Granddad had said about the bottle with the memory in it.

'No,' said Granddad. 'This one's more of a gas. Are you ready?' Granddad asked. They all nodded in silence, and Granddad uncorked the bottle.

POP!

A sparkling whiff of colourful smoke came floating out of the bottle and began swirling all around them. It smelled like sweet fruit and deep rich earth all at the same time. The gang breathed it in.

Immediately, Jack could feel his eyes starting to water.

'It tickles!' Blossom cried with a high-pitched giggle.

Within seconds, the tickling sensation had turned into a fierce prickling one and suddenly Jack's eyes were filled with great flashes of hot fizzing light. It felt like fireworks were exploding inside his pupils and though it wasn't exactly unpleasant, he felt the need to quickly snap them shut as tight as he could … and then, surprisingly, it was all over.

Jack opened his eyes and to his astonishment, everything looked and felt exactly the same.

'Nothing's changed.' he said, trying to hide his disappointment.

'Hey, what's the big idea?' Rocco grumbled.

Granddad couldn't help but giggle to himself. The giggle soon turned into a laugh and the laugh soon turned into a roaring howl! The gang were all watching Granddad as he fell down on to grass and rolled about the floor like he had just been told the funniest joke in the world. 'You should see the look on your faces!' he cried.

'Wasn't something supposed to happen?' asked Blossom, staring around as though she had forgotten something.

'Yes, my darling girl!' said Granddad as he gathered himself, wiping the tears from his eyes. 'It will! It will! But be patient, my dear, and I promise you, it will all become clear!'

Just then, a heavy crack of thunder rang out in the sky above.

'Looks like the storm's beginning to pick up, which means it's time for you boys to head home and get ready. I'll see you all back here, at midnight on the dot. And, Jack, don't forget those keys!'

Granddad led them all down to the end of the orchard where, buried under a horde of twisting vines, Jack could see a pair of tall metal gates. Once more Granddad clapped his hands three times, and the ivy snaked away, and slowly, the huge gates began to part.

'Come on, Terry, let's get you home,' said Rocco as he picked Terry up off the grass and cradled him in his arms like a newborn. 'I'm starving.'

'You're always thinking about your stomach!' Bruno muttered as they wandered off through the gates.

Jack watched the brothers walk away, Dottie trotting along behind. As Blossom chased after them to say goodbye, Jack suddenly realised he was on his own with his granddad for the first time since being in the other world. There were still thousands of questions Jack wanted to ask and they all now rushed into his head as he realised this might be his last chance to ask them.

'How are you going to fix her?' asked Jack in an urgent whisper.

His granddad stared at him for a moment.

'You haven't said anything to her yet,' Jack said. 'When are you going to tell her and change her back?'

'Ah, young Jack, I wish magic were so simple,' said his granddad. 'But don't you worry, dear boy. It is all under control.'

The last thing in the world Jack wanted was to lose his mum again and he could sense a feeling of hopelessness rising up in him.

'Come on, Jack!' shouted Rocco, standing by the gates. 'It's about to start chucking it down!'

'Trust me, Jack,' said his granddad, giving him a wink as Blossom came back towards them.

'See you tonight, kid!' said Blossom, as she linked arms with her dad and the two of them headed back down into the tunnel.

Jack sighed, watching them go. Then he turned around and followed after the Buckleys. What else could he do?

Overhead, dark thunderclouds were gathering and moving slowly across the sky.

'It's gonna be a big storm.' said Rocco, staring upward.

'It's gonna be a big night.' said Bruno.

As they walked back round the side of the old house and turned down the little alleyway that led to their back gardens, Jack could feel his tummy twisting in knots. His head was buried deep in thought and he wondered if he should tell the Buckleys his secret. If he was going to tell them the truth, now was the time. But before he could say anything, the dark clouds opened and it started pouring with rain.

'Quick, run!' shouted Rocco, and the boys all sprinted off towards their houses covering their heads as they went.

'See you later, Jacky-boy!' said Bruno, as they disappeared through their gate.

NEW POWER!

'It's going to be a big one tonight, they say!' said Mr Broom as Jack dried himself off and sat down at the dinner table.

His dad was holding a steaming hot mug of gravy, and the table was all set for dinner. 'It's all they've been talking about on the news today. Stay in! Lock all your doors and windows! You might get struck by lightning, they keep saying!'

'Do you think it's going to be as bad as that?' asked Jack.

'Probably not,' said Mr Broom, smiling. 'They always like to exaggerate when it comes to the weather. It's what they do best!'

He placed the mug of gravy on to the table and sat down. 'I made us sausage and mash,' he said. 'I couldn't find the gravy jug anywhere so the mug will have to do.'

'It's perfect, Dad,' said Jack as he poured some hot gravy over his mashed potatoes and started eating. He was ravenous.

'How did the boys' homework go?' asked Mr Broom as he began tucking in.

'Homework?' asked Jack, then, 'Oh yeah!' he said as he remembered his excuse from last night just in time. 'It was fine. Yeah, we got it all finished in the end.'

'That's great news!' said Mr Broom, chewing away. 'I decided not to go into work in the end. Thought I would buy us some nice food and cook us a slap-up meal instead!'

'So does this mean you're not going back to the animal home?' asked Jack.

'We'll see,' said Mr Broom. 'I'd much rather be spending my time with you. It's time we hung out together more. I only wish I didn't have to leave those poor animals with horrible Mr Nettles. Perhaps we should steal them and bring all the animals here! We could keep them in the garden!'

Jack giggled and, with a small glint in his eye, he said, 'Well, maybe the animals will be OK ...'

Mr Broom sighed. 'Grumpy Nettles doesn't care for them the same way I do. He doesn't care for them at all. He only feeds them water and rotten old vegetables. At least when I was there, they got the odd slice of apple now and then. I'd have to sneak them in, mind.'

Jack paused and sat back in his chair watching his dad. 'You fed the animals apples?'

'Oh yeah,' said Mr Broom. 'They love them! Your granddad showed me that when I first started working there. He used to bring loads of them in and didn't give a hoot what Grumpy Nettles had to say about it. Ah, the good old days! Absolutely marvellous!'

'What was he like?' asked Jack.

138

'Who? Your granddad?'

Jack nodded.

Mr Broom paused for a second, still with a smile on his face. 'Well, he was very passionate about what he did. He loved all creatures and always did right by the animals at the home. He put them first above anything else. Apart from his daughter.'

'Did you trust him?' asked Jack.

Mr Broom looked up sharply. 'Oh, you never knew with that man,' he said. 'No one could figure him out. Not even your own mother. You never knew what he was up to! He was a man full of surprises and unexpected ideas. Whenever you tried to second guess him, he'd pull something completely unexpected out of his sleeve. Yeah, your granddad always had his own plans on the go.'

Jack was listening intently and becoming more and more anxious.

'He loved your mum, though,' Mr Broom added. 'He would have done anything for her. I would have too…' said Mr Broom, his voice trailing away into nothingness.

Jack smiled softly and for a few seconds neither of them spoke as the rain continued beating against the windows outside.

'Oh, I do miss her, Jack,' Mr Broom said. 'Not a day goes by where I don't imagine her walking through that door. Wouldn't that be something.'

Jack wished he could tell his dad everything he knew, but he couldn't. Not till he knew his granddad would make everything right again. They both continued eating in silence. When they had finished, they washed all the dishes together and put them neatly away in the cupboards.

'It's late. You'd better be getting yourself off to bed,' said Mr Broom. 'It's nearly ten o'clock.'

'Is it?' said Jack in surprise. He looked at the clock on the wall and then he stared out of the window. *How peculiar,* he thought, it was still light as day outside.

'That's weird …' Jack muttered to himself as his dad began shuffling him out of the room into the hallway.

'Go on, get yourself on up to bed, young man, and I'll see you in the morning!' said Mr Broom. 'Let's do something fun tomorrow!'

Jack headed up the stairs, still wracking his brain as to why it hadn't turned dark outside. Once he was in his room, he shut the door behind him. He heard a loud THUMP from the wall behind his bed. It was coming from Bruno and Rocco's room. He pulled open his window and looked over to the window to his right. Sure enough, there were Bruno and Rocco, sitting on the window ledge with their legs dangling over the edge.

'It's bizarre, isn't it!' said Rocco. He was still cradling Terry, who was fast asleep in his arms.

'It's so light,' Jack said. 'Why hasn't it gone dark?'

As clear as day, Jack could see a small rabbit go hopping across his back garden. It quickly disappeared off to bed down a small hole in the ground and that's when Jack realised. 'It must be the magic smoke from the bottle!' he said.

'Of course!' said Bruno, slapping his head.

'It's our new power!' said Rocco, beaming. 'We've got night vision!'

'No way!' said Jack.

'Yeah, baby!' whispered Rocco, bouncing up and down on the window ledge. 'I can fly and I have night vision! This is better than Christmas!'

'Did you get the keys OK?' asked Bruno, but before Jack had a chance to answer, a loud voice screamed through the walls of the next-door house. 'I hope you're both in bed up there! I won't tell you again!'

'See you at midnight, Jack!' the brothers quickly whispered and slammed the window shut.

Jack sighed as he realised it wasn't time for bed yet. He still had to find his dad's giant ring of keys.

144

KEY ROBBER

Jack closed his window and crept out on to the landing. Without stopping, he tip-toed past Ozzie, who was napping under the radiator in the hallway. He could hear his dad still clattering away downstairs, so quick as a flash he slipped into his dad's room.

'And where are you sneaking off to?' Ozzie said with a large yawn.

Jack popped his head back out and said, 'I'm stealing Dad's keys to the animal home. We're going to set all the animals free. Make sure he doesn't come upstairs and if he does … stop him!'

Ozzie yawned again and seemed very uninterested as he returned back to his nap.

It was a strange feeling being inside his dad's room all by himself. Jack very rarely went into it alone and whenever he did, it was only to pop his head around the door and see if his dad was home. The room smelled just like his father did and it seemed tidy enough with everything put away in its rightful place. But where were those keys?

As quietly as he could, Jack started scurrying around searching the room.

He opened all the drawers and cupboards but the keys weren't in any of them. He even crawled under the bed and searched but they were nowhere to be found. Then he stopped scrabbling about the floor and had a think. Where would his dad keep them? *In his pocket, maybe,* Jack said to himself. But the giant ring of keys was too big to be kept in any normal trouser pocket. Jack creeped over to the wardrobe and opened the doors. Mr Broom's dirty old overalls were hanging up inside. Jack rummaged through all of the pockets but he still couldn't find them. He began rustling away at all the other clothes that were hanging there in the hope of hearing a jingling of keys, and then he glanced down and finally he saw them. They were hanging off the top of one of his dad's boots. He picked them up gratefully. They were a lot heavier than he'd thought they'd be. There were two sets of keys attached together and there must have been at least fifty keys on each ring.

He was just closing the wardrobe when he heard the sound of footsteps coming up the stairs. His father was coming to bed! Still clutching the giant ring of keys, Jack darted across the floor towards the door and hid behind it. Jack's heart was pumping so fiercely he could feel it in his throat. If he got caught now that would be the end of everything.

That was when he heard his father speak. 'Ozzie, get out of the way,' he heard his dad saying. 'Ozzie, what are you doing? No, don't do that! Ozzie, get outside now!' What on earth was going on? Jack could now hear the sound of Ozzie being scooped up and

Mr Broom's feet stomping grumpily back down the stairs.

'What's gotten into you, Ozzie?' his dad was saying.

Very slowly, Jack peeped round the door. The coast was clear. Jack smiled to himself as he saw a tiny wet puddle on the carpet.

'Thanks, Ozzie!' Jack whispered to himself as he shot back into his room and gently closed the door behind him. He threw the keys down on to his bed and got out his waterproof jacket.

And now there was nothing left to do but wait.

150

NIGHT JOURNEY

Jack thought midnight would never come. But of course it did.

At a few minutes to, Jack sneaked downstairs again and crept out the back door. The rain was still falling and the night air was crisp. But it didn't feel like night-time. Outside was as light as day and it seemed so strange to Jack being able to see everything around him as if it was a bright new morning. There was a fox standing in the middle of the lawn staring at Jack with its shining eyes. Jack had never seen a fox as close as this before. Jack whispered hello and the fox nodded to him nobly and then continued on his way, disappearing silently through the bushes.

With no time to lose, Jack zipped up his jacket and pulled the hood over his head and went sprinting down to the bottom of the garden as fast as he could. He just about managed to stay on his feet without slipping over on the wet grass. He shot straight through the back gate and into the alley behind. When he reached the road at the bottom of the alley, he could feel his whole body tingling with excitement. The rain was tearing down all around him but he didn't care in the slightest. It felt exhilarating. He kept running and running all the way to the tall gates at the back of the old empty house when out of nowhere a blazing light suddenly hit him. Jack squinted through the beams of light and could see the old Beetle still parked in the middle of the orchard with his granddad leaning out of the window.

'I got the lights working!' he shouted, waving Jack over.

Jack headed towards the car. He could see Blossom, Bruno and Rocco all grinning together on the back seat surrounded by apples.

'Squawk!' said little Terry, looking as happy as ever in Rocco's lap.

'We have night vision, kid!' Blossom cried, hopping up and down on the back seat. 'Can you believe it?'

'So what animal was it from?' asked Jack, as he got into the front seat next to his granddad.

'It's from my friend the fox.' Granddad smirked. 'I imagine he's still living around these parts somewhere.'

Jack smiled to himself and said, 'I think I

just saw him in my back garden.'

'Ah, there you are then!' said Granddad cheerily. 'Did you get the keys?'

'Piece of cake!' said Jack, holding them up proudly.

'Well done, my lad!' Granddad cried, slapping the dashboard. 'Come on then, let's not hang about any longer! That storm's right overhead now … it'll be passing over soon!'

Jack reached for his seat belt as Granddad started the engine with a huge BANG! Then the car blasted forward through the tall gates and they were off! Everyone gripped their seats in terror as Granddad tore away at an incredible rate. Jack couldn't tell whether they were having the time of their lives or just utterly petrified as the car shot down the hill. Granddad was cackling away in the front seat like a happy child and pressed his foot down hard on the pedal. 'Hold on to something!' he said as the car accelerated forward faster and faster, zigzagging this way and that through the town.

Billows of smoke blew out the back of the old Beetle like a steam engine as the old beat-up car whizzed through the streets. Jack knew they must be close by now and sure enough, in the distance, he soon saw the glowing lights of the animal home. He glanced down and noticed his hands were trembling. Were they actually about to do this? He felt like he was with a gang of fugitives running from the law. He glanced back at the others. He could see they were in the grips of a big feeling too, and although he was filled with anxiety, in that moment Jack wouldn't have wanted to be anywhere else in the world.

Soon Granddad brought the chugging engine to a stop. They were parked outside the front of the animal home.

'The eagle has landed!' said Granddad.

'I thought you said it was a Beetle?' said Blossom.

'That was the best car ride ever!' cried Rocco.

'Shall we grab some apples?' asked Bruno.

'Fill your pockets!' said Granddad, getting out of the car and popping open the boot. 'We'll save the rest for later! Come on! Everybody out!'

The gang stuffed their pockets with as many apples as they could and headed towards the main gates. Jack suddenly noticed that Rocco was wearing something red which he had pinned round his neck. It was flapping wildly in the wind and seemed to lift Rocco ever so slightly on to his toes. He had a spring in his step, thought Jack.

'Is that a … cape?' asked Jack.

'It's a towel,' Bruno said, rolling his eyes at his brother.

'I think it looks great!' said Blossom. 'I wish I had one!'

'Me and Terry are superheroes tonight, aren't we, Terry!' Rocco said as he took some raisins from his pocket and began feeding them to his little friend. Terry nibbled at them and squawked gratefully up at Rocco. When they got to the gates, Rocco handed Terry to Blossom for a moment, and began clipping a bumbag around his waist. 'This will be perfect, Terry!' he was saying as Blossom handed the baby dodo back and with great care, Rocco placed Terry inside the bum-bag. 'There you go, Terry.' he said. 'You comfy? You'll be safe in here.'

Terry squawked back at him as he nestled down into the bag with his little head poking out the top.

'All right,' said Granddad, 'now if you'll hand me the keys, Jack, it's time to go in.'

With a slightly shaking hand, Jack handed them over. There was a great seriousness about Granddad now as he took back possession of his old set of keys.

For what seemed like a long time, Granddad held the heavy keys in his hands.

'Do you know which one opens the door?' Jack asked him.

'Of course I do,' said Granddad, handing him one of the sets. 'These keys used to be mine. I wrote all the names on them, see?'

Jack looked closely and was surprised to see that on every key was the same slanting handwriting he'd seen written on all the bottles.

'I did it so I wouldn't get them all muddled

up,' Granddad went on. 'Now let's see …
here it is!' He took a key from the other set he
was holding and wiggled it into the keyhole.

The huge key turned with a satifying
CLUNK, and Granddad pushed the gate
open and they all stepped inside.

BREAK OUT!

Once they were in, Granddad closed the
door behind them and turned sharply to
face the gang. He played with the great ring
of keys for a while, separating them out into
two sets. He gave a set to Bruno and a set to
Jack.

'Jack and Bruno, you now both have the
keys you'll need,' he said quietly. 'And I have
the one I need,' he added, holding up one
big key, which Jack assumed must be for
Jumbo. 'I'm going to cut the power now so
the security cameras don't see us. Then I'll
grab Jumbo and meet you back at the main

exit. Good luck. You are a wonderful gang – the best I've ever seen – and I have every faith in you.'

The gang all swallowed nervously and Jack felt a twist in his stomach but he didn't let it show as he nodded back at Granddad.

A moment later, and he was gone.

Rocco took a deep breath and patted Terry on the head. 'This is your first flight, Terry.' he said. 'You're gonna love it, trust me!'

Terry began chirping excitedly and was bobbing his fluffy head up and down inside the bumbag.

'Let's go, then!' And with that Rocco soared up into the sky.

'SQQQQUUUUAWWWWWK!' squealed Terry as for the first time in his admittedly short life so far, he took flight.

Jack and Blossom smiled up at the pair as they zoomed off into the night.

Then with a, 'Good luck, gang!' and another gush of wind, Bruno shot off too.

'Right, come on, kid, let's go!' whispered Blossom as she hurried forward into the grounds. Jack clenched his fists and raced on after her. Together they went charging up the main stretch of the animal home. There were enclosures on all sides and, using his night vision, Jack started unlocking the gates, one after the other.

'Hey, you guys!' Blossom whispered through the bars.

'Who's that?' came a hooty voice above them. 'Where did you two come from?'

Three wise old owls were perched side by side along a metal pole and staring down at them curiously.

'Now just hang on a moment,' another owl said. 'You're children! You shouldn't be here at this hour. Have you lost your parents?'

'No, silly!' giggled Blossom. 'We're

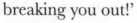

breaking you out!'

'Breaking us out?' the owl chuckled, shaking his feathers. 'Well, well, well, I don't think so, my dear child. I'm afraid you must be mistaken.'

'No, she's right!' said Jack quite plainly.

'We're taking you all to a better place. We need you to head over to the main exit as quickly as you can and wait there for more instructions.'

'Head over to the main exit?' the last owl hooted. 'Well, I've never heard of such a thing!'

'You're gonna love it!' Blossom cried. 'We've got apples and everything!'

'I'm not too fussed about apples,' said one owl. 'Do you have any worms?'

'I'm sure we can find you some,' said Blossom. 'Meet us by the gate and we'll see what we can do!'

'I didn't think about that,' Jack said to

Blossom with a shrug as they raced over to the next gate. Animal heads began popping up all over the place wondering what on earth was going on. Jack and Blossom were calling out instructions to them, and in a short time, there were creatures wandering all over the place.

Jack looked back along the main thoroughfare to see a huge pig the size of a small car trotting in the direction of the gate, making loud grunted snorts

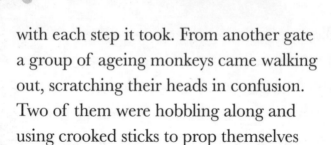

with each step it took. From another gate
a group of ageing monkeys came walking
out, scratching their heads in confusion.
Two of them were hobbling along and
using crooked sticks to prop themselves
up. The huge pig saw one of them and
stopped and the monkey climbed up on
to the pig's back as if he were hopping on
to a bus.

'Look over there, kid!' Blossom cried.
She was nudging Jack with her elbow and
pointing through the crowd of animals
at a tall giraffe up ahead who was
strolling towards them.

'I've been told to head towards the exit?'
the giraffe said, staring down at them.

'It's over that way,' Jack said, pointing
behind him.

'Thank you very much,' said the giraffe
politely, and carried on its way.

'Bruno's letting them out already!' said

Blossom, grinning excitedly at Jack.

The pair raced on, further and further down the main stretch, opening every gate and door they could find. Within hardly any time at all, the gates were all open, and there were animals everywhere. They were all wandering up and down the main path, or swinging carelessly from the gates. Some were singing and telling jokes and there were others who seemed a bit put out by the whole thing.

'They're just like people.' Jack said to himself.

A white llama which looked more like a very tall sheep was nattering away over its shoulder to a family of meerkats riding on its back. Not too far away from them, a wise old bear was rolling about on the grass, happily humming to himself in a daze. A colourful parrot swooped down from the sky and landed on the shoulder of an enormous gorilla. The gorilla seemed to be staring around, looking awfully confused and not knowing what to think or do.

Jack just stood gazing at the curious sight when he heard a voice right behind him say, 'Is this all your doing?'

Jack turned to see an alpaca's head popping up from behind a hedge. He had a huge mop of thick grey hair covering his eyes and a wonky face as though someone had hit it with a frying pan.

'Can you see like that?' Jack asked him.

'Of course I can see!' the alpaca retorted.

He blew a puff of air from his crooked mouth, making his fringe flick upward to reveal his wonky eye. He didn't look very happy at all.

'Why did you choose tonight

to do all this, can I ask?' he grumbled. 'You couldn't have waited for the storm to pass? I'm freezing!'

'How can you be freezing?' said Jack. 'You're an alpaca. You must have lots of fur to keep you warm.'

'Oh, is that so?' the alpaca quipped.

He stepped out from behind the hedge and Jack quickly noticed that there was hardly any fur on the creature at all. He looked completely naked. His tiny body was trembling against the wind and the rain, making him look like a newly born calf.

'Why have they shaved your coat off?' Jack asked him.

'They haven't shaved it off!' the alpaca blurted. 'It's all fallen out! I'm balding! That's what age does to you! Didn't you know that?'

The alpaca then stormed off into the crowds, mumbling things like, 'You youngsters don't know you're born,' and

'You wait till you're my age.'

Jack had to admit, the rain was getting rather heavy now. Another great crack of thunder boomed out of the sky. The air seemed to be growing colder and the trees all around began to sway harder against the wind.

'Hey, guys!' came a voice from above.

Jack looked up and saw Rocco hovering above one of the enclosures.

'What's inside there?' shouted Blossom as they hurried over.

'Flamingos!' shouted Rocco. 'These are the last ones! All the other animals are out!'

Jack and Blossom nodded, and wandered into the enclosure. Beyond a shallow pond, Jack could see four flamingos standing like sculptures beneath a large graceful tree.

'We'd better go and talk to them,' said Jack as they walked over to the pond, Rocco swooping down to join them.

Peering through the giant leaves which were as large as open umbrellas, Jack could see the flamingos all huddled together peacefully in the silvery light.

'Why are they all standing on one leg?' whispered Blossom as they edged closer.

'It keeps the other leg warm,' whispered Jack.

'Does it?' said Blossom in surprise.

'Yeah, my dad told me that,' said Jack as they continued forward cautiously. 'He knows loads about animals.'

'Hey, look what's coming our way!' came a cheerful voice from beneath the tree. 'We've got visitors!'

'Whoever it is, please be leaving us alone,' said another voice sleepily. 'Can't you sees we be resting?'

There was a long pause as the large pink birds gave enormous yawns and ruffled their feathers.

'We've come to rescue you,' said Blossom.

'Rescue us?' the flamingo laughed. 'I don't know if you've noticed, but there's a pretty big storm going on right about now.'

'And besides,' said another flamingo, 'we're all a little too old and shabby to be gallivanting off into the night with the likes of you!'

The flamingos all started laughing and patting each other on the back with their magnificent wings.

Just then, Terry have a little squawk from inside Rocco's bumbag.

'Hang about ...' one of the flamingos said, seeing baby Terry's head poking out from Rocco's pouch. 'What's that you've got there?'

The flamingo at the front slowly lowered its hidden leg and stepped forward. 'Where's you be finding

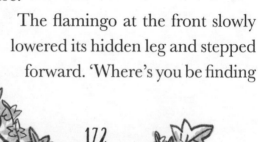

172

a bird like that?' he asked, staring at Rocco.

'What's it saying?' Rocco whispered to Jack out the side of his mouth but Jack didn't answer him.

'We didn't find him from round here,' Jack told the flamingo. 'His name's Terry. We found him in another world. We've come to take you there.'

Immediately, the four flamingos all bowed their heads.

'What are they doing?' whispered Rocco even more seriously this time.

'I think they're bowing.' Blossom murmured, not having a clue what was going on.

'A bird from another world!' the flamingo said, raising his head slowly. 'Well that must be some world, but that be an extinct bird you've got there. And any bird

173

such as this, we be worshipping. That is the way of the law of birds.' All the time he spoke, the flamingo's eyes never left Terry's face. In seconds, the whole atmosphere had changed and the flamingos were all now standing to attention like a team of marines.

'So, you'll come with us?' asked Jack excitedly.

'You just show us the way,' said the flamingo.

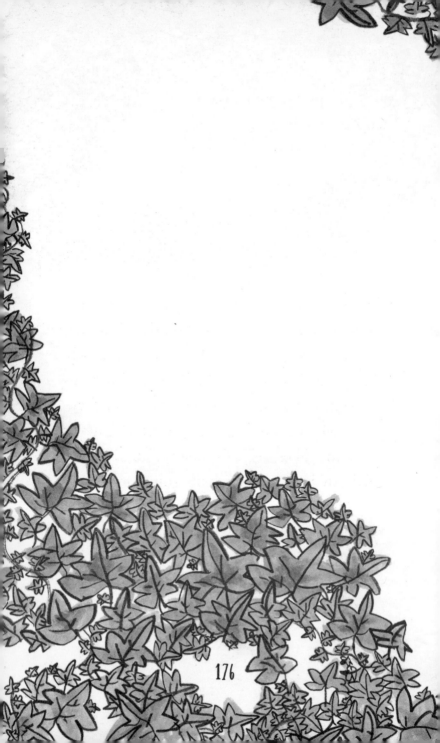

BUSTED

Every enclosure was now empty and the animals were all standing around and looking at each other, confused. Jack listened closely and could hear all the tiny little whisperings of what the animals were saying, and there was a whole lot of stuff like, 'Well, I've never seen the likes of this before!' and 'Does anybody have a clue what's going on?'

'That's all of them, I think!' Bruno shouted as he came whizzing towards them. 'Wow, it's like a zoo in this place!'

'Well, duh!' said Rocco.

Jack smiled and patted his friend on the

back. 'You did great, Bruno,' he said.

'Looks like you did too!' said Bruno, still catching his breath. 'You still wearing that stupid towel, Rocco?'

'It's a CAPE, and for your information, Terry and I are now gods according to the law of birds!' said Rocco, sticking his little chest out as far as it would go. He handed Terry another little raisin to chew on and said to him, 'We did great, didn't we, Terry! We were like superheroes flying up there!'

'Come on, you lot!' cried Blossom. 'We're not finished yet! We need to get them all to the main gate.'

The gang began rushing around madly, calling out to all the animals to get a move on. The enormous gorilla Jack had seen looking confused suddenly appeared behind him and tapped him on the shoulder with its giant finger. Jack turned around in shock and looked up into the gorilla's monstrous eyes.

'Hello …' said Jack with a slight tremble in his voice.

The gorilla was watching him closely and Jack could feel its warm breath against the top of his head.

'I wanted to thank you for freeing me,' the gorilla said kindly.

Jack's eyes widened with surprise. This wasn't the voice he'd expected to hear at all. The gorilla was a female and her voice was gentle and regal. She sounded like an African queen.

'You're welcome,' Jack told her. 'Do you know where to go?'

'I do now,' she said, nodding her head tenderly. 'I asked the warthog. He seems to have a keen sense of direction.'

'That's great!' said Jack and offered her a fresh apple from his pocket.

She took it gratefully and sniffed the apples skin with her huge flaring nostrils. 'Delicious,' she said and went thumping along and up the path towards the exit.

'All right, I think they're all heading in the right direction now. Let's head towards the main gate!' Jack shouted.

The gang were in a whirl of excitement now as they realised their goal was in sight. Rocco was hovering in the air waving them along as Bruno went whizzing around like the fastest sheep dog in the world rounding everyone up. All around them there were creatures all shuffling about and bumping into one another, but they were all going the right way now at least.

Blossom came dashing forward and hopped up on to a large tree stump stuck in the ground. 'Listen up, everybody!' she yelled. 'We all need to get moving towards the exit into the car park outside! It's this way! Everyone follow me!'

All the animals went racing after Blossom towards the main exit and as they rounded the corner, Jack could see the main gate, which was wide open. He was sure they'd closed it on their way in. Granddad must already be there with Jumbo! The plan was working magnificently. Jack was bursting with pride and excitement. He had never known a feeling like it.

He was already celebrating in his head, looking round at his amazing friends, and all the amazing animals, when he noticed … the gate was swinging closed.

Then to his horror Jack saw that the gate was being slammed shut by two security guards.

'Blossom …' he yelled, trying to call out to her, but it was too late. One of the guards had already grabbed her, and the other was shining a torch directly into her face, and just when Jack thought things couldn't get any worse, that's when he saw Mr Nettles.

JUMBO!

Jack couldn't believe what he was seeing. But it was true. There in front of his eyes was Mr Nettles, in his slippers and a dressing gown with bright pink dots all over it, with a face like absolute murder. He looked like he had been pulled out of bed and was clearly not in the slightest bit happy about it. He stared around glaring at the crowd of animals as they all started backing away into the shadows.

The guards were standing behind Mr Nettles, smirking and batting their torches like police truncheons. One was fat and one was thin and they both wore identical uniforms, only the fat one had a baseball cap on his head.

'Who are these chumps?' Bruno growled, clenching his fists. 'Let go of Blossom!'

'Who are WE?' said Mr Nettles in a threatening voice. 'Who are YOU? And what are you doing in my animal home? From this moment on, boy, you can be sure that we are now your worst nightmare! Grab him!'

But they had picked the wrong boy to mess with. As the fat guard went for him, quick as a flash Bruno zoomed out of the way. But it was too late for Jack. The guards seized him, and both guards kept a tight hold on him and Blossom.

'Hey!' Blossom yelled, kicking her legs up into the air. 'Get off me, you big brute!'

'Ooohh, check this one out!' the thin guard snorted, shining his torch in her eyes. 'We've got a little rebel here, haven't we, boss!'

'Leave her alone!' Jack roared as he struggled to free himself from the fat guard's grip.

Mr Nettles bent down to Jack slowly, showing the bottom row of his yellow stained teeth. They were all crooked and his stale breath smelled like an old damp book. 'Well well well! Look who it is. You thought you had us there for a second, didn't you?' Mr Nettles sneered. 'Your stupid little friend might have got away for now, but we'll catch him, don't you worry.' He was glaring at Jack with his hard, piggy eyes and Jack stood there glaring right back at him.

'Why are your eyes bright green?' Mr Nettles snapped.

'Why are you wearing that stupid dressing gown?' Jack snapped back at him.

'We have night vision,' Blossom said

huffily. 'We're *foxes*.'

Mr Nettles stared at Blossom, having absolutely no idea what she was on about.

'What shall we do with them, boss?' said the fat guard sneering.

'I wonder. Should we see what the police have to say about this?' Mr Nettles grinned. His voice was quiet and threatening and his face was now very close to Jack's. 'Or perhaps we should call that useless father of yours? Or better still,' he added with a horrible smile, 'why don't we lock them inside one of the cages and throw away the key.'

'Nice one, boss,' the thin guard chuckled. 'Yeah, let's lock them up and watch the little brats squirm.'

'You're just big bullies!' Blossom snapped at them.

'Yeah and don't you forget it, you little brat!' the fat guard shouted, and just as he did, an apple came falling down from the sky and landed directly on to his head.

'Ouch!' yelled out the guard, and then the other one as another apple came pelting down. The guards let go of Jack and Blossom as they looked up to see who was attacking them.

'Direct hit!' came a cheer from the sky as Rocco came swooping down and stamped on Mr Nettles' head with both of his feet. Then Mr Nettles yelled out, screaming, 'OWWW! What the heck was that!?'

In a flash, Bruno grabbed hold of Jack and Blossom's hands and the three of them darted for cover. They all came skidding to a stop behind a large tree and ducked down.

'Thanks for saving us, Bruno!' said Jack.

'Don't thank me!' Bruno told him. 'That was Rocco!'

Rocco suddenly landed beside them and Blossom squeezed a hold of him as tight as she could. 'You're my hero, Rocco!' she cried.

'Where are you, you horrible brats!' shouted Mr Nettles, as the flashlights searched the darkness for them. 'You might as well come out now. You know we're going to find you eventually, and when we do …'

Just then, Jack heard a strange sound. He pressed a finger to his lips to tell the others to be quiet. 'Do you hear that?' he whispered.

The gang all listened. Faintly at first, but becoming louder and louder each time, a far-off rumbling sound could be heard. It was coming towards them.

Over by the gate, the guards were still rubbing their heads and staring around dimly.

'What's that noise?' the fat guard said.

'Oh shut up, will you!' Mr

Nettles snapped, staggering back up on to his feet. 'Just find the children. I'm going to teach those little punks a lesson if it's the last thing I do!'

But the guards were still staring around them with a puzzled look in their eyes. At first, it sounded like heavy rumbling in the sky. But it wasn't coming from the sky. It was coming from the ground, and it was getting closer and closer.

'I don't like this.' said the thin guard with a shaky voice. 'I don't like this one bit…'

Just then, there came a thunderous roar from out of the darkness.

Mr Nettles and the guards swung round instantly, dropping their torches on to the ground. Then an extraordinary thing happened. A great elephant the size of a bus came exploding out of the bushes with an old man riding on its back.

'It's Dad and Jumbo!' Blossom cheered.

'They've come to rescue us!'

All the colour drained from Mr Nettles' face as Jumbo came marching towards him, making the whole ground shudder. The guards' eyes widened with fear as they watched the tremendous creature's feet hitting the ground each time with the force of a small bomb.

'He doesn't look happy.' the thin guard cried, backing away.

Jumbo roared again and swished his giant trunk through the air. The guards both screamed in horror and went sprinting off through the trees.

Jack just stood there gawping as he watched Jumbo closing in on Mr Nettles, who was so petrified he couldn't even move. He was shaking uncontrollably as Jumbo and Granddad came to a stop, towering over him.

'Let's throw him away, my old friend!'

Granddad cried and, in a flash, Jumbo wrapped his thick trunk around Mr Nettles' whole body and swept him up into the air.

'A marvellous idea,' mused Jumbo. 'Where shall we throw him?'

Mr Nettles was screaming as loud as he could with his legs kicking out wildly in every direction. 'PUT ME DOWN!' he cried. 'PUT ME DOWN!'

The gang by now were all shrieking with laughter. 'Throw him up a tree!' shouted Bruno. 'Throw him in the pond!' shouted Blossom. 'Chuck him in a cage and throw away the key!' cried Rocco.

Jumbo was glaring at Mr Nettles as the ridiculous man flapped away like a newly caught fish. 'OH PLEASE, OH PLEASE!' Mr Nettles was screaming. 'DON'T HURT ME! PLEASE DON'T HURT ME! I'LL DO ANYTHING!'

Ignoring him, Jumbo went

thundering
along up the
path towards
one of the ticket
booths next
to the main
reception.

'Bring us
those keys,
young Jack!'
Granddad called out.

192

Jack ran over to the booth with the gang all chasing after him. He unlocked the door and stood well back as Jumbo tossed Mr Nettles in. Then at a nod from Granddad, Jack locked the door and passed the set back to Granddad.

Mr Nettles crumpled on to the floor, looking only too grateful to be locked away in the safety of the ticket booth.

'I think we've let him off lightly there,' said Granddad, ruffling Jack's hair as they walked back towards the others. 'What a clever bunch you all are!' Granddad beamed around at them.

'I've never seen a real elephant before …' said Rocco, gazing up in wonder.

'This is Jumbo!' Granddad told him. 'He's my greatest friend in the whole universe! We've been through it all together, haven't we, my old friend!'

'We have indeed!' said Jumbo, rising

up into the air on his hind legs. 'It is so magnificent to see you again! After all this time, my dear friend has returned!'

'I promised I was going to come back and take you with me, didn't I!' said Granddad whilst patting the tuft of silvery hair on top of Jumbo's head.

'I can't thank you children enough for bringing him back!' said Jumbo, bowing to the gang gracefully.

'It's nice to see you again, Jumbo!' said Blossom as she reached out, stroking his trunk.

'It's nice to see you too, my dear child,' said Jumbo kindly, 'and you too, Jack.'

Jack smiled and nodded at Jumbo shyly.

'Excuse me?' came a polite voice from out of the shadows. 'Sorry to interrupt but is it safe to come out now?'

The gang all looked over at a zebra who was poking his stripy

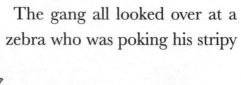

head out of the bushes.

'It's perfectly safe!' Granddad shouted. 'Everyone this way!'

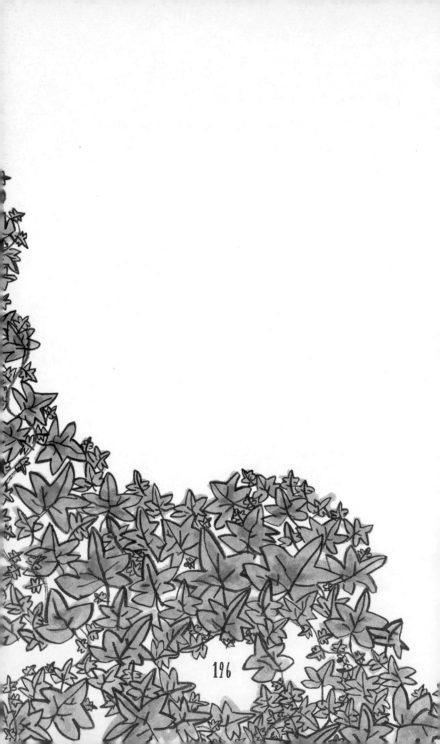

ANIMAL PARADE

Two minutes later, and a long queue of animals were streaming through the exit and out into the empty car park. Jack leapt out of the way and watched an endless stream of animals of all shapes and sizes go hurrying past.

The car park was now swelling with a great flock of wild creatures. They were everywhere. Large packs of them were all huddled together, shielding one another from the blustery winds whilst others seemed quite contented and were strolling up and down looking curiously around at their new surroundings. Great bolts of lightning were flickering silently like gigantic camera flashes overhead as the rain continued to drift down from the clouds.

Jack swept the wet hair away from his eyes and couldn't believe what he was witnessing. He was completely bowled over by the hugeness of the whole thing. But he knew it wasn't over yet. They still had to get the animals to follow them up the hill. The idea that all these animals would just trot obediently up the hill after them seemed completely ridiculous.

'What happens now?' asked Rocco with his towel flapping wildly in the wind.

'Do we just start driving up the hill and hope they follow?' asked Bruno.

'We need to get their attention somehow' said Jack.

Then Jack had an idea. He went racing over to the old Beetle and, making sure he had a few apples left, he pulled himself up on to the bonnet, climbing all the way up until he was standing on the roof. He took a deep breath and cleared his throat.

'We've come here tonight to rescue you!' he shouted. 'We need you to follow us! You need to follow this car full of apples!'

The animals all turned to look at the boy shouting on the roof of the car and shuffled forward as they tried to hear what he was saying.

'Did he say apples?' a voice from the back said.

'Yes, I think so,' said another.

'That's right! You don't have to eat soggy old vegetables any more!' Jack yelled out to them. 'We're taking you to a new home! You'll be safe there! There won't be any cages or people there to lock you away! You'll be able to run and play and you can just be ... you can just do whatever you

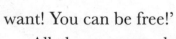

want! You can be free!'

All the creatures began whispering to one another and saying, 'Sounds like a good plan!' and 'Do you think they're really going to share all those apples with us?'

Jack could see Jumbo and Granddad at the far end of the car park ushering out the last few animals and pulling the enormous gate closed behind them. Granddad was carrying a sloth under his arm who seemed to be fast asleep. He came weaving through the enormous crowd of faces that were all smiling warmly at him.

The animals were all calling out, 'Hello, Herbie!' and 'Where have you been all these years? We missed you.'

'It's wonderful to see you again!' Granddad was saying as he made his way over to the car.

The gang watched and smiled as

Granddad carefully placed the sleeping sloth into the passenger seat and buckled him in.

But some of the animals had now turned away again, and begun talking amongst themselves.

'Apples are all very well, but it's so wet and cold out here. At least my cage is dry,' said one, as slowly the small crowd began to turn back towards the main gate.

'Keep going, Jack!' his granddad said. 'You were doing great!'

'Listen up, everyone!' Jack shouted. 'I know some of you are tired and wet and cold, but if you'll just come with us, we will take you somewhere where it NEVER rains, where there are no cages, and definitely NO Mr Nettles ... just follow this car, and these delicious apples! Trust us!'

And just like that, the tide in the car park began to change. The animals that had been heading back to the main gate were now shuffling closer to the car.

Jack then called out to the Buckleys. 'OK, we need to go now while we have their attention. Bruno, stay at the back of the line and keep a close watch! Make sure you round up any stragglers! Rocco, you and Terry keep a view from above and make sure no one gets left behind!'

'Got it!' the brothers yelled, taking up their positions.

'Are you ready?' Jack said to his granddad, jumping down off the car.

'Ready when you are, Jack!' shouted Granddad from wheel.

Jack turned to see Blossom staring at him with an expression he had never seen on her face before.

'Who taught you to become such a leader?' she said.

Jack smiled. 'You did,' he said.

She gave him a great big hug and said, 'Let's go!'

'You two will have to jump in the boot, I'm afraid!' Granddad told them as he popped open the boot full of apples. 'I've put all the stragglers in the back!'

Jack and Blossom looked through the window and saw a car full of sleeping creatures, all huddled together on the back seat. There were dozy opossums and sleeping koalas and even an enormous python who was taking a nap and had wrapped himself into a giant ball.

'I'm glad we're not in there,' Jack said as he pulled the boot open and sat himself in amongst the apples, legs dangling over the edge. 'I'm not too keen on snakes.'

'Aren't you?' said Blossom, seating herself beside him. 'I think they're fantastic! They're all hissy and slithery!'

'Ready?' shouted Granddad from the front.

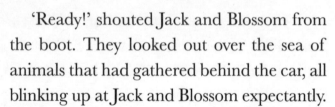

'Ready!' shouted Jack and Blossom from the boot. They looked out over the sea of animals that had gathered behind the car, all blinking up at Jack and Blossom expectantly.

Jack tossed out a couple of apples. 'Plenty more of these if you follow us!' he said.

The animals licked their lips and shuffled closer.

'Right then!' said Granddad as he started the engine. 'Let's get going!'

An almighty bang came firing out the back of the old Beetle. The animals all jumped backwards into the air, as Granddad shifted the gears into first.

'Sorry!' shouted Granddad. 'OK, off we go.' And the car moved forward, and they were on their way.

Jack and Blossom started dropping the apples one after the other on to the ground and watched with huge smiles as all the animals began picking them up.

'It's working!' said Blossom, grinning at Jack. 'They're following us! We did it! We really did it!' She grabbed Jack's hand and squeezed it tightly. Jack's heart swelled as he smiled at her and squeezed it back.

The little car moved on through the quiet town. All the shops were closed and the curtains were drawn, as you'd expect given it was the middle of the night. The endless rain meant the streets were completely deserted too. There were no cats sitting on walls or lone foxes crossing the road. The entire town seemed to be tucked away in hiding.

But then, very slowly, faces with curious looks on them began popping out from behind drawn curtains. More and more windows lit up as the parade of animals travelled past. Front doors began to open as people appeared in their dressing gowns and stared out in shock. Neighbours were turning to each other and shrugging their shoulders, looking baffled beyond belief, as the old Beetle chugged on past followed by a long line of wild and exotic creatures. At the back of the line, there was Jumbo, looking mightily pleased and waving his trunk at all the confused little faces staring up at him as he strolled by. Everyone must have thought the circus had come to town.

During the next half-hour, the streets would be lined with hundreds of bewildered spectators, all

standing in the rain. Children everywhere
would run out into their front gardens
wearing their pyjamas and pointing at the
parade of animals
in wonder.

The parents would come scrambling out after them and stand there gaping too, wondering what on earth was happening. Nobody in the town had ever seen such an incredible sight as this before. And they never would again.

It was the wee hours of the morning but Jack was not the least bit tired. It was all too exciting. The rain was coming down harder now and a great rush of water came flowing down the hill along the gutters and into the drains. Jack was grateful for the open boot covering his head.

'We're getting close!' shouted Blossom over the cracking thunder, pointing towards the crest of the hill ahead of them. 'I can't wait to be in the other world with Dad and all the animals! I'm going to ride on Jumbo's back all day long and then we'll go swimming in the river together and he'll spray me with his trunk!'

With every word Blossom said, Jack's excitement and happiness began to drain away and a panicked sense of doom came over him. It was a horrible prickly feeling. It filled his stomach and churned around in there relentlessly. It suddenly dawned on him that he might be about to lose Blossom for ever. He had no choice. Once they reached the top of the hill, there wouldn't be time. He had to tell her his secret now.

'I have to tell you something!' Jack shouted as flashes of lightning exploded with thunderous booms above them.

'What did you say?!' Blossom yelled, cupping her hands over her ears as another deafening crack of thunder rang out in the sky.

'I HAVE TO TELL YOU A SECRET!' Jack cried out.

'OHH, I LOVE SECRETS!' Blossom shouted excitedly. 'WHAT SECRET?'

Jack stared back at her, trying to think how to put it. He didn't want to have to shout it, but it was so hard to hear anything over the tremendous storm. Great cracks of lightning continued flashing all around them and the thunder was banging from all sides.

'It's just, the thing is …' Jack started nervously, but then he realised Blossom wasn't listening. She had turned around and was staring up the hill with her mouth hanging open.

'Look, kid!' Blossom said pointing. 'It's the doorway! It's opening up!'

Jack looked to where she was pointing and saw the old house, high up on top of the hill, bathed in a beautiful shimmering light.

Jack knew that light. It was the light of the other world.

MR BROOM'S FURY

At last the car arrived at the top of the hill and pulled up by the alley that lead to the old empty house. Granddad turned off the engine and in that exact moment, as if by magic, the rain began to clear and the rumbles in the clouds became quieter and quieter and the storm slowly began to drift away over the hill.

Granddad leapt out of the car. 'Hurry!' he shouted. 'We haven't got much time!' He called out to Jumbo who came thundering up to the car with his great pounding feet. 'Clear a path for us, Jumbo!' Granddad

211

yelled. 'We need a clear path from the alley to house, and up those stairs!'

'Leave it to me!' said Jumbo, who went crashing down the alley and through the rusty old metal gate like a tank. He pulled away the ivy tunnel in one big sweep with his enormous trunk.

Jack and Blossom hopped out of the boot landing in the soaking wet mud and ran through the gate to watch. They were soon joined by Rocco and Bruno.

'What's he doing?' said Bruno as Jumbo went slamming through the front door of the old empty house, taking it clean of its hinges and causing some of the front wall to fall down in the process.

'He's making the entrance clear so everyone can get through!' cried Granddad cheerfully. 'He's like a bulldozer once he gets going!'

Shielding his eyes, Jack could now see

straight through from the front of the house, up the stairs and into the entrance hall. With one more crash from Jumbo, who was by now inside of the house, the wall that separated the back room from the entrance hall came down too, and now they could all see straight through to the back wall - the ivy-coloured doorway to the other world. The wall was now sparkling with golden light, just as it had been when Jack had walked through it, only the day before.

It was an incredible sight - like a doll's house with the front wall removed - and a huge elephant crashing around inside.

'All clear!' shouted Jumbo, and Granddad began ushering all the animals up the steps of the old house and off into the light.

'That's it everyone! Head straight up the stairs and into the lights! You're almost there! That's it, keep moving!'

Blossom and the Buckleys were stood watching in awe, but Jack knew he couldn't just stand there. Time was running out. He had to confront his Granddad once and for all. He couldn't just let him take Blossom away. He summoned up all the courage he had left inside him and marched straight up to his Granddad.

'She still thinks she's going into the other world with you!' said Jack trying to keep his voice down, so Blossom didn't hear. 'When are you going to tell her? I thought I could trust you! You can't just go! You have to change her back!'

'One moment, young Jack!' his Granddad said as he carried on waving the animals through.

Jack stumbled backwards as the long line of animals came strolling past between them. There were just so many of them. There were hobbling monkeys and a limping camel and emu's and penguins and horses and lemurs and even a hopping kangaroo.

'Which way is it to the other world, please?' a llama asked Granddad looking a little confused. 'I'm a tad deaf and didn't quite catch all that?'

'Straight ahead, up the stairway and into the light,' Granddad said pointing the way. 'You can't miss it!'

A burning hot bubble of rage was now bubbling away in the pit of Jack's stomach. 'You're a liar!' Jack shouted and just as he was about to shout some more, a voice even louder than his came booming down the alley. 'Would someone mind telling me what on earth is going on!?'

Jack's heart stopped.

It was his dad.

'Jack?' he said, marching straight towards

him with his eyes bulging out of his head on stalks. 'What in blazes are you - are all these animals – what are they all doing here? I… I don't even know what to say… You are in big trouble, young man!'

Mr Broom was becoming more and more agitated and clearly didn't have a clue what to say or how to process what was happening, and just as Mr Broom looked like he was about to explode, he spotted Granddad. His mouth fell open, all words gone. He was staring at him as if hypnotized.

'Oh, hello, Albert!' cried Granddad waving to him. 'I didn't see you there! It's quite a sight, isn't it?'

Mr Broom couldn't believe his eyes and gave his face a good old shake as if trying

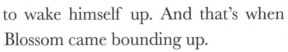

to wake himself up. And that's when Blossom came bounding up.

'Is this your dad, kid?' Blossom cried as she came skipping over.

When Mr Broom saw Blossom, he turned as white as a sheet.

'So nice to meet you, Jack's dad!' she said, putting out her hand to shake his. 'My name's Blossom and this is my dad!' she said, slapping her dad on the back.

For a few seconds Mr Broom just stared at her. His whole body had become limp and Jack wondered if he was going to faint.

'But, how–' Mr Broom mumbled to himself. 'It's not possible…'

'Anything's possible, Albert.' said Granddad with a little glint in his eye.

Mr Broom seemed to wake up at this. He snapped his head towards Granddad, and began advancing on him with a most serious look on his face.

'What - is - going - on?' Mr Broom said in a slow and terrifying voice. 'You disappear for SIX YEARS. My wife too. Neither me nor Jack have any idea what on earth happened to either of you and then you suddenly turn up, out of nowhere, all smiles, with no explanation.'

Granddad sighed and patted Mr Broom gently on the arm.

'OK, Albert, you're quite right,' he said. 'It's time I gave you some answers…'

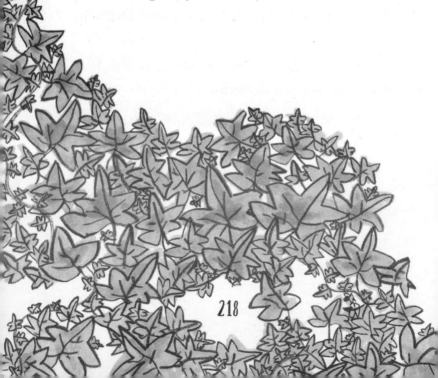

THE TRUTH

'The last big storm was just like this one,' said Granddad. 'That was six years ago, as you say. You kids won't remember it,' he said smiling down at Jack and Blossom and Rocco and Bruno, 'but I certainly do! I'll never forget it! Great blasts of thunder shook up the whole house and all my bottles came crashing down, spilling magic all over the place. Then came the pouring rain and all this remarkable ivy started growing.' He gazed down at Jack and Blossom looking more serious than ever. 'Then a doorway appeared,' he said. 'A doorway to another world, and I'd never known a feeling like it. I had such a powerful yearning to see what was inside.'

Jack and Blossom were staring at Granddad, listening intently to every word, Mr Broom too, flicking looks between Granddad and Blossom.

'Before I went through, I wrote a note for my daughter,' Granddad went on, 'telling her I would be back… and then lightning struck and the doorway opened. I walked through to the other world and soon discovered that there was no way back. Not until the next storm came. The doorway was closed. I was stuck there. I spent many months trying to get home but there was no way. It was impossible. I'm not saying it was a horrible place to be stuck, far from it, but I did so want to be able to come back and explain and then take my animals with me.' Granddad knelt down in front of Blossom and looked at her through those bright twinkling eyes of his. 'You must have come looking for me, Blossom. But instead of finding me, you found this bottle.' From his pocket Granddad produced a small bottle. It was the one the gang had found that first day in the house, with "*Blossom at the bakery. Age nine.*" written on the label.

'That was the bottle I found in the house!' cried Blossom. 'It has my name on it!'

'Yes, it does!' said Granddad. 'And what was inside it was very special. But also very dangerous'

'Why was it dangerous?' asked Blossom.

'It was dangerous because the magic inside it turned you into a little girl.'

'What do you mean?' said Blossom with a frown of confusion. 'What do you mean, *turned* me into a little girl? I AM a little girl!'

'Inside this bottle was a memory of yours,' Granddad said to her. 'A most brilliant and perfect memory from when you were nine years old. I always dreamed of making an invention like this one. Jumbo had been helping me. I was trying to capture the elephant's power of remembering, trying to find a way to bottle up one beautiful moment so one day you could relive it all over again as if it was happening for the very first time.'

Jack couldn't take his eyes off his Granddad as he spoke.

'You see Blossom,' Granddad said softly, 'I bottled this memory for you to keep but I failed to realise how powerful the magic inside it was. An unimaginable magic that would not only bring back that memory of being nine years old and eating cake for breakfast, but would turn you back into that child, and erase all the memories you'd made since.'

'I... I don't think I understand...' said Blossom stammering a little. Jack's heart was aching for her. He had never seen her stammering and confused.

'I know, darling,' Granddad said softly. 'How could you? It's hard for me to understand too. I guess some magic is just too mysterious. Or too dangerous.' His eyes flicked up to Mr Broom who was standing there lost for words.

'I'm so sorry, Albert,' said Granddad, hanging his head. 'I'm sorry to all of you.'

Granddad looked sadly at Jack, then looked back into his daughter's troubled eyes. 'Just know you did nothing wrong, Blossom, and the fault is mine,' said Granddad. 'And now it's time to fix it.'

'I am still coming with you, aren't I?' asked Blossom.

Granddad motioned for Jumbo to come over, then looked down fondly on his daughter, his eyes shimmering with tears. 'I have decided to go alone,' he said with some difficultly. 'I'm an old man now and I can't go on forever. But you, my dear child, you have a life ahead of you, and you need to be with your real family.'

'But you're my family!' said Blossom, not understanding.

Granddad winked at her and pinched her on the chin. 'Of course I am,' he said. 'And I always will be. But you have another family now too.'

Blossom looked up as an enormous shadow suddenly came spilling over them. Jack and Mr Broom took a step backwards as Jumbo came right up to Blossom. He smiled at her fondly, with great big watery eyes. He looked at Granddad, and Granddad nodded, and with just the tip of his trunk, Jumbo wiped away one of his tears and then placed it softly against Blossom's cheek.

'Look…' Jumbo whispered, turning Blossom round to face Jack and his dad, 'and remember.'

Blossom stared at Jack and his dad. For a few moments she looked so confused, and then, very slowly, her head started tilting to one side as if she was remembering something, and her eyes began to grow wide.

Jack and Mr Broom watched in astonishment as the tear Jumbo had placed on her cheek started to glow. It was growing too, bigger and bigger, until eventually there was a soft golden glow all around her.

And then, to everyone's amazement, Blossom began to transform right in front of their eyes. Her legs were getting taller and her arms were getting longer. It was all happening so fast. She kept growing and growing until suddenly, she wasn't a little girl any more. She was a woman. A young woman with long fiery red hair.

Mr Broom fell to his knees.

'No way...' whispered Bruno. 'She's a grown up!'

'Well, I didn't see that one coming!' gasped Rocco.

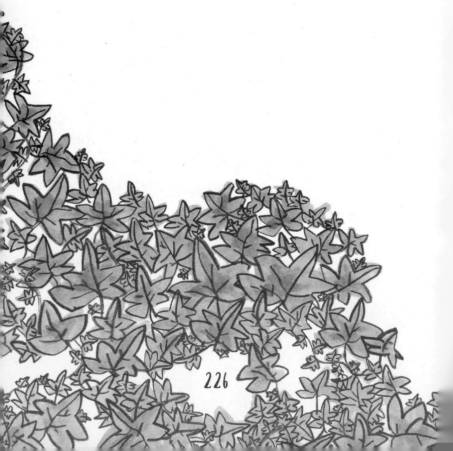

FAREWELL

Jack stared at the woman in front of him, his eyes wide and filling with tears. He couldn't believe she was standing right there! It was his real mother. The mother who he'd never really known. The mother who he'd so longed to see for all these years. And now she was here, he had no idea what to say to her.

'Anna?' said Mr Broom getting to his feet, and coming towards her slowly.

'Hello, dear!' she said with a huge smile. Mr Broom laughed and cried as she came over and hugged him. 'Oh, it's so wonderful to see you! I feel like I haven't seen you in…'

227

Her voice trailed off, as she stared around with a confused look on her face.

Everyone else stood watching open-mouthed to see what would happen next.

'Oh, THERE you are dad!' said the woman as she spotted him. 'I've been searching the whole house looking for you! Where have you been all this time? I've been so worried!'

It was then that she saw Jack standing there, staring at her with tears in his eyes.

'Jack?' Mrs Broom whispered. 'W-why are you crying?' And as she said it, her eyes began to glisten too.

'You've grown so big, Jack,' she whispered, coming towards him, and stroking his arm, as if she wasn't quite sure he was real.

Jack wiped his eyes and tried to think of what to say, but he was just too astonished to speak. Tears were spilling from his mother's eyes now as she pulled Jack into her arms.

Jack held on to her as tightly as he could, his eyes squeezed shut.

'What's happened to this place?' she asked as if suddenly noticing her surroundings. 'Where on earth did all these animals come from?'

Jack suddenly noticed that all around there were animals staring at them with wet eyes. One of the monkeys handed a ripped piece of cloth to a sobbing pig and everyone stood back as he blew his nose.

'We're freeing them all!' said Rocco. 'Don't you remember?'

Mrs Broom turned round when she heard the familiar voice and almost burst into the air when she saw who it was.

'Rocco!' she cried. 'Oh look, and little Terry! And Bruno! There you are! I do remember! I do! We did free all the animals, didn't we?'

'We sure did!' Granddad said coming over with a huge smile on his face. 'And now it's time for me to get back.'

'You're leaving?' asked Mrs Broom taken aback.

'Look at you,' said Granddad placing his hands on her shoulders. 'My little girl, all grown up! I want you to know that I am a very proud father and you've given meaning to my life that I had no right to expect.'

Mrs Broom wrapped her arms around her dad and embraced him tightly.

'Now don't you be worrying about me,' said Granddad patting her on the back. 'I want you to promise me that. Because it's all going to be alright. You have your family now and I have my animals. Everything's going to be OK.'

Then Granddad stepped away, and came and stood in front of Jack.

'It's been a terrific honour, young man,'

he said. 'I don't think you'll ever understand how much this has all meant to me. Albert? Here are your keys!' he said, tossing the giant set to Mr Broom. 'Not that you'll have much use for them any more!' he said with a wink, then he whispered to Jack, 'though you might be interested in the little gold one… It's the key to my secret basement, should you ever need it…'

Granddad winked at the astonished Jack who was smiling up at him.

'Thanks for, you know, everything,' said Jack, who was still a little lost for words.

Granddad ruffled his hair and began shooing all the animals towards the house before walking over to the Buckleys.

'And goodbye to you both, you wonderful boys!' he said. 'I hope you had fun.'

'Oh we did!' said Bruno.

'It was amazing!' said Rocco. 'I always

wanted to be a superhero!'

'Well today you were,' said Granddad, 'you both were.'

Then suddenly from inside Rocco's bum-bag came a loud 'SQUARWK!'

'Is that little Terry, I hear?' said Granddad, bending down to where Terry was, still nestled inside Rocco's bum-bag, and giving its head a little stroke.

Rocco took a step back, and Granddad straightened.

'Do you think…' said Rocco, 'do you think Terry could stay here with me?' he asked pleadingly. 'I'll take extra good care of him! I'll build him a big old hutch in the garden and feed him warm milk every day!'

Bruno rested a gentle hand on Rocco's shoulder. 'Terry needs his mum, Rocco. He needs to get back to his world.'

There was a short silence and then Rocco gave a big sigh. A sadness had come over

him that no one had ever witnessed before. Jack could see in Rocco's eyes that he didn't want to give Terry away.

But Rocco bravely lifted Terry out of his pouch, gave him a little kiss on his furry head, and carefully handed him to Granddad. 'Will you make sure Terry gets back to his mum, safe?'

'I'll see that he does,' said Granddad softly.

'Goodbye, little Terry,' Rocco sniffed. 'You're going home to your real mama now! You be a good boy and don't let the other dodos pick on you when you get back. One day you'll be stronger than all of them!'

'Squawk!' said Terry, looking back lovingly at Rocco as Granddad smiled at Rocco, before turning away and heading towards the doorway.

A curious silvery glow was now coming from the entire house, and from the back wall in particular. All of the animals had gone through the doorway now, except for Jumbo, who was waiting for Granddad at the top of the stairs. The silvery light from the other world was streaming out from the doorway like flowing water and as Granddad began to climb the stairs, everyone came forward to wave him goodbye.

When they were right in front of the light, Granddad and Jumbo turned back. Jumbo bowed his head and waved with his trunk, and Granddad blew one final kiss to his daughter.

Jack wrapped one arm around his mother's waist and the other around his dad's and watched as very slowly, the magnificent glowing light faded away and Granddad, Jumbo and Terry disappeared into the other world.

MORNING CAKE

The Brooms and the Buckleys began to walk slowly away from the house and into the alley behind, none of them quite sure what to say.

Jack smiled as he saw Bruno chuck an arm around Rocco's shoulder. 'You've got real guts you know,' Bruno whispered to his brother.

Rocco flicked him an inquisitive look and said, 'What are you talking about?'

'I'm talking about you,' Bruno said. 'You were really brave. Saving us all from those nasty guards, handing Terry back without

237

making a fuss. You were right. You WERE a superhero tonight.'

Rocco frowned up at his brother, no doubt waiting for the punchline, thought Jack. But even Jack could see Bruno meant it.

'Thanks,' said Rocco with a small smile, when suddenly the moment was disturbed by an ear-piercing shout.

'Rocco and Bruno! What do you think you're doing out of bed? Get back in the house this SECOND!' she yelled. 'Where on earth have you been?'

Mr and Mrs Buckley came marching down the alley towards them, with Dottie scampering along behind them.

'You have no idea how much trouble you're in!' said Mr Buckley sternly, while trying to keep his dressing gown from falling open. 'We've both been sick with worry!'

'But Dad…' Bruno began.

'Your mum's been going out of her mind!'

shouted Mr Buckley. 'Home now, the pair of you!'

'Don't be too hard on them,' said Mr Broom walking over, arm in arm with Mrs Broom. 'They've been real champions tonight, helping Jack with some animals in need.'

The Buckley parents stared at Mr Broom disbelievingly.

'I'm Albert, I live next door,' said Mr Broom shaking both their hands. 'And this is my wife, Anna,' he said, smiling across at her.

'We haven't had a chance to meet yet,' said Mrs Broom, who seemed to be stifling a laugh.

'Oh, right, yes well, it's good to finally meet you,' said Mrs Buckley, sounding not quite sure of herself.

'Jack's been telling me all about your boys and how they've been getting on with their summer homework,' said Mr Broom with a smile. 'What good boys they all are!'

While the grown-ups talked, the Buckleys came over to Jack.

'Hey Jack!' whispered Rocco excitedly, 'I can't believe Blossom's your MUM!'

'Yeah, what a cool mum to have!' said Bruno. 'I wish ours was like that!'

Dottie came rushing over and licked Jack on the hand. 'Hello, Dottie!' he said grabbing hold of her and giving her a big squeeze. 'We missed you tonight.'

Dottie wagged her tail and barked and barked. And that's when Jack realised - he couldn't understand a word. 'My powers have gone.' he muttered.

'No way! Let me try...' said Rocco as he leapt up into the air and landed back down again with a thud. 'Oh you're kidding me!'

'How come our night vision is still working

then?' asked Bruno.

'I think that's just the sun coming up,' Jack said pointing out over the horizon. 'It's nearly morning.'

'So, we're normal again?' said Rocco.

There was a brief silence as the boys all stared at each other not knowing what to say.

'Say your goodbyes you two, and let's get you back home,' said Mrs Buckley as her and Mr Buckley said their goodbyes to Mr and Mrs Broom.

'See you a bit later on?' said Bruno.

'You bet,' said Jack.

'Come on then, Rocco!' said Bruno punching his brother in the arm. 'Last one to the gate's a LOSER!'

Before Rocco had a chance to catch up, Bruno raced on up the alley shouting back, 'Night, Blossom! I mean… Mrs Broom!'

Jack couldn't help smiling to himself as he watched the brothers go tearing off, Dottie trotting happily behind them, Mr and Mrs Buckley clearly having no idea what to make of it all.

So that was that. The adventure was over. Everything on the hill had become very still and when Jack turned around, he could see his mum and dad holding each other, and smiling. Out in the distance, the sun was beginning to rise in the early morning sky. A soft orange haze of light was glowing beneath the rim of the horizon and turning all the clouds into the colour of delicious pink candy floss.

Jack walked up behind his parents, slid his hands into theirs and they all turned to watch the sunrise together. They had been standing there for quite some time when Mr Broom finally spoke.

'Probably best not to tell anybody about this,' he said.

'Yes, we'll keep it as our little secret,' said

Mrs Broom, smiling down at Jack and giving his hand a squeeze.

Jack smiled and squeezed it back.

They were all quiet for a moment. Then Mrs Broom said, 'I'm famished!'

'Me too!' said Jack, his stomach grumbling loudly.

'Let's go out for breakfast!' said Mr Broom.

'I know!' said Mrs Broom, looking across at Jack, her eyes twinkling excitedly. 'How about… cake!'

'Yes!' shouted Jack.

'For *breakfast*?' Mr Broom laughed. 'Well, why not…'

The birds had started chirping to one another as the sun continued to rise and all Jack could hear was the pleasant tweeting of birdsong. The streets shone with rain and sunlight and Jack felt like the luckiest boy there ever was as the three of them linked arms and strolled down the hill towards the bakery.

245

AUTHOR Q&A

1. There are a lot of animals in your books. What animal would you be and why?

I would have to be the Vogelkop superb bird-of-paradise. Not only can it fly but this bird can also flip its cape and dance!

2. In *Jack's Secret Summer*, Jack, Rocco and Bruno all get powers from drinking magic potions. What magic powers would you like?

I think flight would be a really fun power to have. To see the world from such a different perspective would be incredible. It would be interesting to play around with the power of invisibility and I would love to be able to travel through time.

3. Why did you want to become a children's author?

I love inventing new worlds and characters where there are no limits to story-telling. I find a lot of joy in remembering my own life as a kid and I am able to really see the world through the eyes of my younger self. It's very freeing and to me there is nothing more exciting than that.

4. What was your favourite children's book?

It was Matilda by Roald Dahl. It was the first book that I really connected with as a child.

250

JACK'S SECRET ACTIVITY!

1. Think of your favourite animal.

2. Think of the best superpower and give your animal that superpower! For example, a cat that can breathe under water, or a mouse that can fly!

3. Draw a picture of your super-animal.

4. Write a short story about your super-animal's adventures!

Jack Ryder was cast in the role of Jamie
Mitchell in *EastEnders* at the age of
sixteen – a character he played for
five years. He then moved into
theatre, performing in plays by
Alan Bennett, Tim Firth and
David Hare, before going on to direct
the West End productions of *Calendar Girls*
and *The Band* musical. It is his lifelong
ambition to be a children's book author.
Jack's Secret World is his second book.